BURN FOR ME

Into The Fire Series

J.H. CROIX

This is a work of fiction. Names, characters, businesses, places, events and incidents are either the products of the author's imagination or used in a fictitious manner. Any resemblance to actual persons, living or dead, or actual events is purely coincidental.

Copyright © 2017 J.H. Croix

All rights reserved.

ISBN-10: 1546562656

ISBN-13: 978-1546562658

Cover design by Cormar Covers

Cover Photography: FuriousFotog/Golden Czermak

Cover models: Chase Ketron, Hannah Nicole

No part of this book may be reproduced in any form or by any electronic or mechanical means, including information storage and retrieval systems, without written permission from the author, except for the use of brief quotations in a book review.

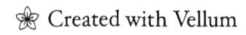

❀ Created with Vellum

To second chances in life & love!

Sign up for my newsletter for information on new releases & get a FREE copy of one of my books!

http://jhcroixauthor.com/subscribe/

Follow me!

jhcroix@jhcroix.com
https://amazon.com/author/jhcroix
https://www.bookbub.com/authors/j-h-croix
https://www.facebook.com/jhcroix

BURN FOR ME

One alpha man.
One bossy woman.
A fire that won't die.

Once upon a time, Amelia was my everything. Until I lost her. Now I have a second chance, and I want her back.
She's never forgiven me for something I didn't even do. I've never forgiven her for believing the worst.
One look and the years apart go up in smoke. She's all I ever wanted. A snappy attitude and the nerve to bring me to my knees.
We have seven years of bitterness tangled up between us.
Yet, I can't stay away.
The fire burns too hot. She'll be mine. For keeps this time.

*This is a full-length standalone romance with a guaranteed happily-ever-after.

Chapter One

AMELIA

I shoved through the door into the bar, coming to a quick stop as my eyes adjusted to the light. I brushed a wet lock of hair off of my cheek and threaded through the tables to the bar at the back. Once I slipped onto a stool, the bartender spun to face me. He was a jolly looking man with round blue eyes.

"I'm Tank. You look like you could use a drink," he announced, his wide smile softening his observation.

"A beer will do," I replied.

"House draft okay?" he asked.

At my nod, he spun around. Within seconds, he'd handed me my beer and silently offered a clean towel. Though it was tiny, seeing as it was a bar towel, I quickly scrubbed it over my dripping wet hair and face before handing it back to him. I settled in to try to forget my shitty day.

A bit later, I drained my beer and glanced around the bar, savoring the anonymity of being in a crowded bar in Anchorage, Alaska where no one knew me. I was tucked in the corner by the wall, pleased to have a nice view of the crowd and yet go unnoticed by just about everyone there. Tank caught my eyes again, a question held in them. I nodded and held my empty pint glass aloft. He nodded in return while he mixed a drink for someone and pulled another pint for me with his free hand. The extent of my conversation with anyone this evening had been limited to Tank's earlier introduction.

If he thought anything awry with the fact I was wearing a wedding dress splashed with mud, he didn't show it. Neither did anyone around me. Anchorage was just large enough of a city people left you alone if you appeared to want to be left as such. That said, people were friendly too. Alaska, despite its sprawling geography, kept its residents close, all bound by the knowledge they lived on the edge of the wild and had the strength and guts for such a life.

I took a drag on what was my third beer and wondered if perhaps I should slow down. I was definitely tipsy and on my way to drunk. I fingered the cream silk of my wedding dress. Or maybe I needed to consider it my not-wedding dress. I'd been all dressed and ready to go when I'd failed in my battle against the knot of tension balled like a vise around my heart. I swallowed against the rush of emotion that rose inside as my eyes traveled down the fitted bodice of my dress and bounced to the muddy splotches all over its swirling skirt. Oh yeah. I hadn't simply ditched my groom-to-be just before we got to the altar, I'd bolted in the rain. Another swallow of beer, followed with a slow sigh. What stung the most—all I felt was relief. Not regret, not second thoughts. Just pure relief.

I'd walked across the hallway at the back of the church and barged into Earl's dressing room. There he'd stood, tall and handsome with his dark blonde hair and brown eyes. It was what I never saw in his eyes when he looked at me that pushed me to tell him I couldn't marry him. When Earl looked at me, I saw a kind regard, a humored attempt to appreciate me for who I was. Yet, there was never anything close to the hot fire I'd known once upon a time with someone else. I'd apologized, but I'd also been flat pissed with him for trying to trick himself and me into thinking he really loved me.

A dash into the late afternoon rain on a cool summer day in Alaska had felt cleansing. Until I got chilled and finally ducked into this bar. I didn't even know what it was called. I suddenly recalled I didn't have a penny on me. It wasn't like I'd been carrying a purse for my aborted walk up the aisle. Oh well, oh hell. I caught sight of my reflection in the mirror behind the bar and bit back a sigh. My amber hair was a damp, tangled mess.

I didn't think much about how I looked. To be honest, it was more that I tried not to. I was as tall as most men. I ran my own construction business to boot. I tried to never let it show, but when it came to my femininity, seeds of doubt were planted firmly inside. It didn't help that all but one man treated me pretty much like a man, Earl included.

I gave my head a hard shake and glanced around the bar again, scanning the collection of people. Businessmen rubbed elbows with fishermen here. Sports reigned supreme on the televisions screens mounted at various points in the bar, and a few pool tables were clustered in the corner. That's what I'd do. I loved pool and was pretty damn good at it.

A few minutes later, I was paired up in a game with three other guys. They'd thrown a few looks askance at my wedding dress and seemed amused at playing with me. Tipsy and deep into my *don't give a damn* mode, I set out to beat them.

Roughly an hour later, I grinned as my last ball rolled neatly into a pocket corner. "Well, boys," I said, glancing among them.

The boys in question had been drinking and gotten steadily more sullen as we played. One of them, a hulking sort with dark eyes and hair, glared at me. They'd bet on this game after the first two, and I was due five dollars each from them.

Mr. Hulk, as I'd come to call him in my head, stepped close to me, too close for comfort. "No fiver from any of us. You got that?"

I was just drunk enough not to care. I stretched up to my full five foot eleven inches. He might have more bulk than me, but I was a hair taller. "Ah, I see. You only like to bet if you're gonna win? What an ass," I said, my lips curling in a sneer.

I was stretched too thin emotionally with white hot anger, a simmering anger I'd kept buried for the entirety of the two years I'd wasted on Earl, and a tad too drunk to be reasonable right now. When the jerk stepped closer and put his finger on my chest, I didn't even think. I punched him, right in the nose.

"You fuckin' bitch!" he shouted as he swiped his sleeve across his face, smearing the blood from his nose on his cheek.

He hauled off and punched me back, his fist bouncing under my eye. He had enough heft to send me tumbling to the floor, an inglorious heap of muddied silk spilling around me. I was just tipsy enough not to care that my face was throbbing. Without the mud, minus the dingy hardwood floor under me and definitely minus the crowd now gathered around, I considered the way the silk of my dress spilled in a near perfect circle would have made a great wedding photo—one of those candid shots people would love.

In a flash, Tank was there, shoving the guy who'd punched me away. Voices above me collided with each other.

"Dude, she hit me first!"

"Self defense..."

"Yeah, but she's a girl..."

"She's a fuckin' giant, and she can hit. She's no girl!"

I closed my eyes and wished I could crawl into a hole. The buzz that had kept me afloat this afternoon and evening dissolved into mortification. The jerk was right. I was a giant and no one would ever look at me and think girly thoughts.

"Amelia?"

My heartbeat came to a screeching stop and then jump-started with a hard kick. I'd know that voice anywhere. Through the jumble around me with Tank leaning over to ask if I was okay, that voice rang like a loud bell inside. One man. Only one man had ever looked at me with heat in his eyes, heat so hot it singed me. That man spoke my name now. I didn't have to open my eyes to know. I did anyway. Because I couldn't bear not to see him.

Cade Masters stood at the edge of the circle gathered around me, another man in a bar crowded with men. Shaggy dark brown hair, green eyes, and a body of raw muscle stood before me. My heart felt as if it had been split open. I'd loved Cade in that wild headlong way that only youth allowed. No more than seven years had passed since I'd seen him, but it felt like forever. Cade had broken my heart and walked out of my life when I was twenty-two. He hadn't just broken my heart, he'd betrayed me.

Anger flashed hot and high inside, yet I couldn't look away. My eyes ate Cade up. He wore faded jeans, the fabric so worn it hugged his muscled legs like a caress, and a denim jacket over a black t-shirt. He had something of an outdoorsy, biker vibe. Once upon a time, he'd taken me on long rides on his motorcycle through the nearly empty highways in Alaska surrounding our hometown. He stepped through the crowd and knelt at my side, his green gaze coasting over me. "You okay?" he asked.

I nodded without really thinking about it. He lifted a hand and ran the backs of his fingers along my cheekbone. Oh right, some guy had just punched me in the face. Cade's presence had wiped my mind clean of everything else. With barely a brush of his touch, my heart fluttered and heat tightened inside.

"You sure?"

I swallowed, suddenly aware of my throbbing cheek. My entire day flashed through my mind. A gloriously shitty day. I fought against the tears, but they welled up, unbidden and beyond my control. One tear rolled down my cheek and then another and another. Of all the times and places to encounter the one and only man who still held a piece of my heart, this had to be the absolute worst.

Cade's eyes never left mine. Something flickered deep in the depths of them, but I didn't know how to interpret it. Without a word, he slipped his arm around my waist and lifted me up, bundling me into his arms as if it was the most normal thing in the world to do. "Let's get you out of here," he said and started to stride away.

Tank caught him by the arm, and Cade glanced to him. "Yeah?"

"Just making sure she's okay," Tank replied.

All I could do was nod. I was so totally *not* okay, but I was okay in the sense Tank was asking.

Tank's warm gaze held mine, this bartender who barely knew me, but had somehow known I'd had a bad day and just needed to be left in peace while I had a few beers. I should've stayed put in my seat at the bar. My raw emotions and crazy day, all of my own making if I was being honest with myself, had gotten me into this mess.

"You want the police involved?" Tank asked.

I shook my head and finally found my voice. "No. Let's call it even. I punched him, he punched me."

"You know this guy?" Tank asked next, nodding to Cade.

"Uh huh. It's okay. He's an old friend of my family's. No need to worry," I managed. On its face, my explanation was true. Cade and I had grown up together in Willow Brook, Alaska. Our families had known each other for years. Yet, my explanation left out so much of what Cade meant to me, it was almost laughable.

Tank released his grip on Cade's arm and let us be. Cade was quiet as he strode through the bar, the crowd parting around him. I could only imagine how we looked—me in my dirty not-wedding dress and him giving off his usual *back the hell off* vibes. It was a shock to see him for the first time in years and even more of a shock to be held in his arms. I felt at home in his strong embrace. He held me easily. He always had. I loved that about him. Cade was a good four inches taller than me at six foot three inches and had never cared about how tall I was. He pushed through the door of the bar, stepping out into the late evening. The rain had stopped at some point during the long hours I'd been hiding in the bar.

He paused once we were outside on the sidewalk and glanced down, his gaze catching mine. "Why are you wearing a wedding dress?"

That was Cade, never one to waste time on preliminaries. I'd loved that about him. Oh how I'd loved so many things about Cade, back before he'd left my heart bruised and battered. Right now, I couldn't seem to recall the pain. All I knew was it felt so good—so, so, so good to be with him.

Chapter Two
CADE

"I was supposed to get married today. I didn't," Amelia said.

I stared down at her and tried to collect my thoughts into something sensible. But there was nothing sensible about me when it came to Amelia Haynes. Right now, in fact, I was wondering if maybe I should carry her down the street to the courthouse and marry her. I wanted to. Damn did I want to.

The only thing holding me back was the memory of the look on her face the last time I'd seen her. She'd walked in on her former best friend trying to kiss me in bed. It didn't matter that I'd been turning away and had been plain horrified to wake up and find Shannon climbing into the bed naked. No, what mattered was Amelia saw Shannon mashing her mouth against mine and then acting like it had happened before. Amelia's face had gone white and then dark with fury. I never got another chance to talk to her. Nothing ever happened with Shannon, but Amelia iced me out of her life. The whole situation was made worse by the fact I'd been about to leave Willow Brook, Alaska for a year a week later. Not enough time to make things right.

The emotional upheaval hadn't helped me think clearly. I'd left Willow Brook for my planned year with a hotshot firefighting crew in California and mostly stayed away ever since. I'd returned to Willow Brook a few times to visit my family, but I'd never seen Amelia. At first, it was because I was pissed. She'd shut me out so completely. By the time I got around to thinking maybe I should try to at least make some peace, she was dating Earl Osborne by then. I'd bitterly accepted it was probably best to let it go. No sense in stirring up the past.

I was in Anchorage now because I was taking care of a few errands before driving to Willow Brook tomorrow. I'd accepted a job as a foreman on a hotshot crew based out of Willow Brook. I was finally moving home because nowhere else felt like it for me. I'd hoped I was over Amelia, but one look at her and she gutted me.

I stared down into her eyes and tried to think. Her eyes were like honeyed cognac. Her hair, amber flecked with gold, fell in tousled waves around her shoulders. It was a mess really. All of her was. Her wedding dress was dirty, a bruise was forming on her cheek just under her eye, and I was pretty sure she was drunk.

She stared back at me, and I realized I hadn't said a thing since she made her announcement. "You were supposed to get married today?"

"Yup." She nodded forcefully. "Sure was. I walked out. Couldn't do it. You know why?" she asked, a mulish tone to her question.

"Why?"

She poked me in the chest with her index finger. "It's all your fault."

I was lost, I truly was. How could it be my fault she didn't get married?

"Amelia, I don't know what you're talking about," I finally said.

She rolled her eyes and sighed dramatically. "No one

looks at me the way you did. That's the whole problem. Why'd you have go and be such an asshole?"

While I was reverberating at what she said, she kept on talking, the words spilling out every which way, here and there a word slurring. "Earl tried, oh he tried, to act like it mattered, but he was like every other guy I dated. Not that there were that many. I'm too big. I'm not feminine enough. It's like he thought he could prove he was a man by dating me. Stupid, stupid, stupid." She punctuated these words with a thump of her forehead against my chest, all the while I stood frozen on the sidewalk. Traffic rolled by and pedestrians stepped around us.

Her eyes whipped up again, lasering me with an accusing glare. "You weren't like that. But after it all, you were."

Anger rose inside. She'd boxed me out of her life so effectively, I'd never had a chance to even tell her what *didn't* happen with Shannon. I looked down at Amelia and started walking quickly, driven by the lingering anger at what tore us apart and the fresh anger at what she said about herself. She kicked her legs against mine.

"What are you doing?"

I couldn't answer because I didn't know. It so happened my truck was parked just ahead. I kept walking and stopped beside it, easing her down. The moment her feet landed on the sidewalk, she tried to push away, only to stumble. I reached for her reflexively, catching her fast against me. A bolt of need hit me. Amelia was tall and strong with generous curves. Just as before, my body knew what it wanted. I'd always loved how she stood nearly level with me. My eyes canted down of their own accord to see the soft curves of her breasts mounding up over the fitted top of her wedding dress. I had to force my gaze up and found hers wide and locked on me.

A familiar electricity arced to life. This was Amelia. This was us. Nothing had faded between us, if anything, it burned hotter than it ever had. In a distant corner of my mind, I tried to tell myself not to do this. If I wanted to make things right, I had to go slow. Yet, with her held against me and her amber eyes flashing fire, I did the only thing I wanted. I backed her against my truck. "You're not too big. Don't ever say that again," I growled before crushing my lips to hers.

It was as if no time had passed, well except for the fact I was pouring seven years of longing into our kiss. She arched into me and threaded a hand roughly into my hair, moaning in my mouth with every stroke of her tongue against mine. I couldn't stop kissing her. She felt so good, so damn good. My mind fuzzed out and all I knew was the feel of her against me. A horn honked nearby, and Amelia tore her lips free.

I opened my eyes, my heart pounding so hard, I wouldn't have been surprised if I cracked a rib. Her head fell back against my truck. She closed her eyes, her breath heaving. Her fingers loosened in my hair and her palm slid down to rest over my chest. After a moment, she opened them.

"What was that?" she finally asked over the pounding of our hearts.

"I never stopped missing you."

Chapter Three
AMELIA

I came out of sleep suddenly, my eyes flying open. Darkness greeted me. I didn't know what the hell I'd been dreaming about. For months now, I'd been having anxiety-fueled dreams. Every so often I'd remember them, but they weren't reality-based. The last one I recalled had involved me falling out of a plane in the sky. They'd started not long after Earl and I had finally settled on a wedding date. I should've known right away what they meant. I'd been a bundle of anxiety and nerves about the impending wedding and had known deep inside I didn't want it and neither did Earl. Well, I couldn't speak for Earl. What I knew was I didn't feel much from him. Having once experienced love—the wild, thrumming kind—and passion—the out of control, burning yearning kind—I'd known we were about to miss out big time.

I couldn't remember where I was and suddenly became aware of the body beside me. My eyes gradually adjusted to the dark room, and I could make out the smudgy outlines of the basic furniture in the hotel room. The body behind me? Definitely not Earl. I knew this with certainty because the man was curled up around me and I could feel a rather impressive erection against my bottom. Earl tended to sleep flat on his back. In fact, I couldn't recall a single time when he'd spooned with me. My mind gradually flickered to life from its slumber.

Cade Masters. Here. With me. In bed. The muddled anxiety of my dreams morphed into the most confusing string of feelings I'd ever experienced. It felt so, so, so, so good to have Cade curled up around me. If I thought about it, which I didn't like to do, Cade was the last man I'd been with who'd been affectionate like this with me. He'd almost always touched me—no matter where we were. If we were in public, he had an arm over my shoulders, or my hand held fast in his. In private, well...we'd been young and foolishly in love. We'd snuck off every chance we could get before we were eighteen. After that, we hadn't bothered with sneaking. In bed, we slept just like we were now—with him snugged up behind me, one of his strong, rugged hands resting on the curve of my belly.

It felt so good to have him here, so good it was dangerous. On the heels of how good it felt, I felt sad. Again. I'd made a mess of yesterday. I'd tossed my phone into a ditch somewhere along my meandering walk through Anchorage after I'd dashed out of the church. I hadn't wanted to answer anyone's calls. I must've walked for a solid hour before I ducked into the bar where Cade found me. Oh God. I bit back a groan. I'd started a fight. If anything represented how angry I was at the state of my life, that fight did. I'd hurt Earl, but he hadn't played fair with me either. I didn't know what he thought he'd get out of marrying me, but he didn't love me. Not the way Cade once had.

Correction—not the way I thought Cade once had. That old bitterness twisted its knife in my heart. I'd lost two of the most important people in my life in one day—Cade and my former friend, Shannon. I'd been out of town for the weekend. I couldn't even recall why. I'd returned to the small home I shared with Cade to walk in and find Shannon—completely naked—climbing into bed with him and kissing him. Aside from all the obvious reasons why that hurt like hell, it was all made worse by how Shannon just happened to be the girly, gorgeous girl all the guys chased after when we were in high school. It got under my skin to see Cade with her, and I'd never been able to shake how small I felt in that moment.

In the years since, I had plenty of reasons to reconsider whether I might have misinterpreted what happened, but in the end, all I knew was crushing pain in my heart and burning anger.

I lay still and tried to suss out if Cade was awake. It didn't matter that seven years had passed. I knew the way he breathed when he slept, and he was definitely asleep. With his rock hard cock pressing into me, I didn't dare move, but holy hell, I was turned on. I could feel the moisture at the apex of my thighs. I might be confused, but my body sure as hell wasn't. If my body had its way, I'd wiggle my bottom and roll over and straddle him. I swallowed and tried not to go there in my mind, but I couldn't help it. The mere thought of having Cade inside of me again nearly made me frantic with need. My pulse was racing, my low belly clenched and my channel throbbed.

My recollections from last night after Cade kissed me senseless on the sidewalk were vague. I'd definitely been drunk. By the time I threw my punch at Mr. Hulk, I'd probably had another three beers on top of the three I'd already downed. I remembered Cade helping me into his truck. Next thing I knew, he'd bundled me into his arms and carried me to the elevator at this hotel. This after I almost fell on my face on the entrance stairs.

I had no memory of getting out of my wedding dress, but I wasn't wearing it. I fingered the edge of the t-shirt I was wearing. Cade's shirt. The scent of him surrounded me and made my heart clench. Suddenly, I was blinking back tears. I should've cried yesterday when I dumped Earl. Instead, I was swamped in emotion now and none of it had anything to do with my former fiancé. Every feeling rocking me now was linked to the man curled up behind me. I swallowed against the tightness in my throat, doing my damnedest to get a grip.

I had to get up somehow and get the hell out of here. I couldn't face Cade. Not like this. Not when all I wanted to do was cry and the only person who might be able to assuage the hurt was Cade. I carefully shifted, incrementally moving toward the edge of the bed. It was the hardest thing I'd done in, well, since I'd stormed out of his life seven years ago. The only thing that had made it a tiny bit easier was I'd been so driven by anger and hurt then, the combined force had propelled me away.

Right now, my longing to wrap myself in Cade's warmth and strength and pretend like seven long years of bitterness had never happened was so powerful, it was a pure force of will to move at all. Just when I managed to inch a little bit further, Cade moved. His palm slid across my belly and over the curve of my hip. The calloused skin of his hand sent sparks skittering under the surface of mine. He was all man—every inch of him, including his hands. Even before he'd left for training to become a hotshot firefighter—one of the most physically demanding jobs there was—he'd been nothing but raw, rugged and pure masculinity, a man on octane fuel. I wouldn't have thought it possible, but he was more mouth-watering than ever now. I might be a tad fuzzy in my recollections from last night, but I hadn't forgotten looking up at him in the bar. My heart gave another squeeze. The Cade I'd once known had been reserved, but I hadn't missed the distant, guarded look in his eyes when I first looked into them.

His palm kept moving, sliding into the dip of my waist and coming to rest under the curve of my breast. My nipples tightened, a wash of need rolling through me. He had to be asleep. Right? On the heels of another deep breath, I started to move again and suddenly felt his breathing change. Oh shit. My incremental movements away had been erased when he moved. My bottom was pressed firmly into his hard cock. My channel throbbed, and all I wanted was to give into the wild, burning need I'd never forgotten. When sex with everyone else had paled in comparison—nothing even came close—it was hard not to want to give in. Nigh impossible, really.

My skin prickled with awareness as I sensed him coming awake. He held still, but I could feel the thrum of tension in his body. Hot all over, I pondered how to gracefully get out of this mess when all I wanted to do was straddle him and forget everything else. He might've kissed me last night, but he'd gotten distant afterwards. I remembered that much.

Oh hell. I wasn't going to be a coward. I rolled over, swiftly enough to dislodge his hand from where it was cupping my breast. The moment I rolled over and opened my eyes... Oh. My.

In the smudgy darkness, I couldn't see much, but a light had been left on in the adjoining bathroom, its light filtering across the bed. Just enough for me to see him and just enough to make me nearly melt. His gorgeous green eyes slammed into mine, his gaze, dark and intent, scanned my face. For a flash, I felt lost and alone. The Cade I knew was hidden behind his impenetrable gaze. I could hardly breathe, my pulse skittering wildly.

To say I didn't know what to say might be the understatement of the century. After a few beats of silence, the air around us weighted with seven years of hurt and obviously failed attempts to move on, he pushed up onto an elbow. His hand had slipped onto my belly when I rolled over, and his thumb moved in idle strokes. My senses narrowed to the thin strip of flesh under his thumb, slivers of fire radiating outward. Just a soft brushing back and forth, and I was about ready to lose my mind. My breath was shallow, and my thoughts scrambled.

I clung to my sanity and swallowed. "Cade..."

He saved me. "Amelia, we don't need to talk now. Okay?" he asked, his voice gruff with sleep.

"Okay," I managed, mostly because I had no idea what else to say.

He eased off of his elbow and adjusted the pillow under his head. His eyes were still on me, and I couldn't look away. Years of unspoken feelings crowded the space between us. I sensed Cade knew I was unsettled. Once upon a time, he would have teased me and jostled me out of this place in my head. That was then, this was now. He didn't move away, but he was quiet.

After another few beats, he spoke. "Go to sleep, Amelia."

He lifted a hand and brushed the tangled hair away from my face. On a sigh, I closed my eyes. The tension knotted in my chest eased slightly as I relaxed into this space with him —even with him guarded, I felt *right* when I was with him. Just myself. I drifted off to sleep.

Chapter Four
CADE

I took a sip of coffee—a double shot in the dark, just what I needed. Two shots of espresso in the already rich brew from the diner were enough to nudge me out of my muddled state. Amelia sat across from me, one elbow on the table while she flipped through the menu. She was wearing one of my t-shirts and a pair of jeans she'd picked up at the department store near the hotel. Sporting a black eye and looking tired and out of sorts, she was so damn beautiful it took my breath away. I took a gulp of coffee, needing the bitterness to anchor me.

The sun glinted in her amber hair, gilding it with gold. Last night had been, well, maybe the hardest night of my life. I wanted Amelia—so fiercely, it was an ache I couldn't assuage. She'd been just drunk enough to test my limits. She didn't appear to recall she'd sashayed out of the bathroom last night, after unceremoniously yanking her wedding dress off, and straddled me where I'd been resting in the bed. Propped up on the pillows, I'd gritted my teeth and roughly set her aside. I might want her like I'd never wanted anyone, but I wasn't about to take her when she was drunk and on the heels of walking out on her fiancé. I'd gathered bits and pieces of what happened. In short, she'd dated Earl, never loved him and didn't believe he loved her. Apparently, she'd missed me the whole time.

Even now, I was still trying to wrap my brain around that. Amelia was a passionate woman. She didn't do anything in half-measures, including anger. She'd iced me out of her life so completely, I couldn't quite believe she'd missed me the whole damn time. I'd sure as hell missed her. Yet, I was also pissed. Seven years of being shut out and never once had she given me a chance to explain that absolutely nothing had happened with Shannon. Much as I wanted to erase the time in between, I couldn't. I didn't even know if what I felt was really something. Was it just the echoes of what once was? Maybe I simply needed to get her out of my system, once and for all.

Amelia closed her menu and glanced over at me, her cognac eyes searching my face. My heart clenched so hard it hurt. Amelia was...well, she wasn't an easy woman. She was so strong on the outside—tall, leggy and powerful, she exuded confidence and an innate power. Yet, behind that strength was a soft side.

Oh fuck. I couldn't look at her and not go all crazy inside. Even worse, I was still sporting an erection. Had been pretty much since I'd picked her up off the floor last night. A mechanical release in the shower this morning hadn't done the trick. I couldn't be around her and not want her. I might not be full on like I'd been when I woke up beside her, but my cock was at half-mast and had been ever since I'd laid eyes on her in a tumbled mess in her muddy wedding dress on the floor.

Another gulp of coffee, and I realized I'd almost drained it. I caught the waitress's eyes and held my cup aloft. She nodded from a few tables away. I glanced back to Amelia and decided I'd better figure out how to talk to her. No matter what happened with us, I was moving back to Willow

Brook to stay and it'd be best for us both if we could find peace.

"So..."

I stared over at her. I'd meant to start off with something blunt, maybe even harsh. But my gaze landed on the purple, reddish skin around her eye and saw the pain flickering in the depths, and I just couldn't. I could only drift but so far on the tides of bitterness. She was Amelia, the one and only woman who'd ever gotten to me. No matter how angry I was she never gave me a chance to explain, I'd loved her so hard once upon a time. The echoes of that love—in all of its wild, tangled glory—were still ringing inside. I also knew perfectly well why she'd been so pissed at me.

Hell, I'd almost lost my mind when I heard she was engaged. I couldn't even stand to think she might be with anyone other than me. Thousands of miles of distance between us, and the only way I'd managed to deal with any of it was to shove everything away.

After Amelia had walled me out of her life almost instantly, I'd tried in vain for a week to talk to her. I could be as stubborn as her, so by the time my flight rolled around, I left Willow Brook behind, plenty pissed and bitter. Being able to walk into an intensely demanding year of training and stay on in a job where I often worked so hard I could barely think served to help me forget Amelia. Or trick myself into thinking I had.

I couldn't help but wonder if my biggest mistake had been in actually leaving Willow Brook. Time and distance had allowed me to put off revisiting the ghosts of the lies Shannon wove around us. Hell, had I been around, at some point Amelia would've had to have talked to me. But I'd spent the last seven years flying in and out of the wilderness all over the place. Wherever the worst fires were, I went, along with my hotshot crew.

Now, I was back in Alaska and here to stay. Amelia sat before me, and I'd completely underestimated the hold she had on me. Beyond the fact she could easily intimidate any man, what with her height, her strength and her ballsy attitude, she held my heart in her hands and always had.

"So, don't suppose you have a car somewhere around here?" I asked.

Amelia's cheeks flushed as she shook her head. "No. My mom drove me here because, well, because we were supposed to fly out to Hawaii today."

Of course. She had a honeymoon planned. The very idea of Amelia going on a honeymoon with anyone other than me nearly made me want to pound someone into a wall, but I took a breath and kept it together.

"Right. Should I drop you off somewhere? Do you need to call anyone?"

Her cheeks flushed deeper. "I threw my phone away. Look, I know this is weird, but could you just give me a ride to Willow Brook and drop me off at my brother's place outside of town?"

She wanted a ride? Sweet Jesus. I did *not* know if I could do this.

Chapter Five
AMELIA

I rubbed the hem of Cade's t-shirt between my fingers. His scent surrounded me and threw me full force back into the tumult of my feelings for him. My eyes canted in his direction. His truck was, well, it was what I'd have expected him to drive. It was a black light-duty truck and decked out with every imaginable high-tech feature, yet also battered and worn. He didn't have a nimble, four-wheel truck for show. Cade was a man who used the hell out of his vehicles. He was no cardboard cutout alpha man—he was as rugged, mouthwatering, and alpha as a man could get.

In the seven years since I'd seen him, he'd gone from young, rough and wild to all man—raw, rugged, and so damn sexy it nearly set me on fire. He carried a sense of danger with him and a hard edge. I could only imagine the life he'd led. I'd spent seven long years trying to shove every thought about him far out of my mind. The only thing I'd succeeded in was refusing to listen to anything anyone had to say about him. In a town the size of Willow Brook, that was no small feat.

Willow Brook was situated roughly forty-five minutes

outside of Anchorage with Denali, the highest mountain peak in North America, rising tall in the distant vistas. With its proximity to Anchorage and Denali National Park and Preserve, Willow Brook was a tourist draw for the hordes of tourists that descended on Alaska the minute the brutal cold blew away with the spring winds. As such, Willow Brook catered to the tourists with a mix of restaurants and shops.

I pondered how I was going to explain any of what had happened with my wedding and quickly shoved those worries away. Sadly, I didn't have much to say other than the truth. The more pressing concern was what to do about Cade. Fat lot of good it had done me to block out any and all gossip about him. All I knew was he'd left for California as planned for his hotshot firefighter training and stayed on the crew there. He'd offered little else since he'd scooped me up off the floor last night.

A rush of emotion rose inside my chest. Dammit. I felt like an idiot. I'd cried last night in the shower after Cade unceremoniously shoved me off of his lap. I'd been good and drunk, but I couldn't seem to forget my foolish display. Aside from our initial kiss—which he'd started, dammit—he'd pulled back. Questions flew through my mind. I was starving to know more. Fuck it. I might as well ask. I had nothing to lose.

I glanced his way, and heat coiled low in my belly. His profile was stark against the bright blue sky outside the driver's side window—strong cheekbones and a blade of a nose with a slight bump in it. I remembered the afternoon he broke his nose. He'd gone mountain biking with his friend John and tumbled off when his front tire bounced off a boulder. Just thinking of that made my heart clench. I knew just about everything about him growing up. Even before we'd started circling each other in high school and then started dating, he'd been entwined in my life. His family lived nearby. To this day, his mother Georgia was close with mine. That had made it awful hard to avoid news about Cade, but I managed it somehow.

My eyes landed on Cade's hand, hooked loosely over the steering wheel. Strong with a scar winding in a graceful curve over the base of his thumb, I recalled the feel of his hand on me when I woke in the night. I tore my eyes free and swallowed. This was incredibly inconvenient. Sweet Jesus. I hadn't thought it possible, but I wanted Cade more than ever. A mere day after dumping Earl right before he stood in front of the altar, I was lusting after my ex. The very ex who'd betrayed me.

I'd had to get used to bumping into Shannon around Willow Brook for a few years, but Shannon had since moved to Anchorage, a huge relief. Dealing with Cade's betrayal had been bad enough, but he'd been blessedly gone. Seeing Shannon had been like jagged glass in a wound. Even worse, our circle of friends had been caught in the middle. The scars ran deep, and to this day, I harbored lingering hurt over the friends who'd declared they couldn't take sides.

With a mental shake, I brought my focus back to now. Cade was here and he'd kissed me senseless last night. I'd never been a coward and I wouldn't be one now. "So how long will you be in Willow Brook?" I asked.

Cade glanced my way, his green gaze catching mine and sending my belly in a slow flip. "I'm moving back."

I felt as if I was falling, my stomach dropping out and my heart beating so fast I could barely breathe.

"What?" I finally managed to ask, my voice coming out raspy.

Cade had looked back to the highway, but his eyes flicked my way quickly and back forward.

Tears pressed at the backs of my eyes, and my chest felt tight. My heart felt like it had been scored deeply, the pain stinging and sharp. I'd so effectively buried my hurt behind walls of anger I was surprised at its ferocity now. Cade being almost a ghost in my life had made it possible for me to keep the walls intact. The surprise of seeing him had sent them tumbling down to rubble and now I was picking my way through, wondering how the hell to pull myself together again. He was moving back? I so totally could *not* deal with this.

I stared blindly out the window, completely forgetting I'd attempted to start some kind of a conversation with him. The morning had been hard enough, but I'd had things to do, like get dressed and stuff my muddy wedding dress into a bag the hotel receptionist had politely offered me. Now, I watched the landscape roll by. It was midsummer in Alaska with fields of lupine waving purple in the wind. Denali rose tall in the rear view mirror, while lakes and rocky ledges flanked the highway winding toward Willow Brook.

Cade approached a stop where the highway intersected with another. I could feel him glancing in my direction, the feel of his gaze practically burning a hole in the back of my head. Fighting my tears, I couldn't bring myself to look at him, so I stayed silent and stared out at the view blurred by my tears.

"Amelia?"

I swallowed against the tightness in my throat, but I couldn't manage to respond. He turned onto the smaller highway leading toward Willow Brook and immediately pulled over into a scenic view location off the side of the highway.

Confused, I glanced over my shoulder. "What are you doing?"

He turned the engine off and looked over at me. "We might as well hash things out now. I mean, I'm back. To stay. We have to be able to stand to see each other. Don't you think?"

My heart felt like it might crack a rib, it was pounding that hard. *Pull yourself together. This shouldn't be that big of a deal. Did you think Cade would stay away forever just because it was easier for you?* Actually, I hadn't even allowed myself to think about that. It hurt too much.

I gulped in air and stared back at him, scrambling to gain purchase in my mind. I felt off balance and caught in a riptide of emotions I'd staved off for years.

Cade stared back at me, his gaze direct and unflinching. A mess inside, I fell back on what got me through our break up before—anger.

"There's nothing to talk about," I said, almost cringing at my bitchy tone.

He arched a brow and leaned back in his seat, never once looking away. I couldn't have felt more of a mess if I tried. I had a black eye, wasn't even wearing my own clothes, and had encountered Cade at probably the worst possible moment I could consider. Seriously. I would've had to try to pick a worse time.

"Since you're still pissed at me, I'm guessing you never bothered to figure out that nothing happened with Shannon and me. Maybe you don't want to talk about it, but you asked me for a ride, so I figure you at least owe me a chance to clear the air."

I felt like I was falling again, hurtling through the air with the ground racing up at me. "What?"

"Just what I said. You know, you seem to think you've cornered the market on who gets to be pissed off. I had nothing to do with Shannon. I…"

I started to cut him off, but his glare was so dark, I snapped my mouth shut.

"Did you ever even try to find out the shit Shannon pulled?" He shook his head and kept going. "I don't know what her fuckin' deal was, but she stirred shit up. You walked in as shocked as me when she showed up. You never stuck around to see me shove her away, or to hear the bullshit she spewed. I. Never. Did. Anything. So while you were busy thinking I screwed you over, I got to wonder why you couldn't be bothered to find out it might not have been what you thought," he said, his tone dark and laced with hurt.

He finally snapped his eyes from mine and looked out through the windshield. I sat there stunned, my mind spinning and my gut churning.

"You mean...?"

He swung back to me, lasering me with his gaze. "I mean just that. You iced me out so fast, I never got a chance to explain. I'll admit I was such a fuckin' mess after you bolted and blew me off for a whole week. I steered clear of trying to talk to you about this because, well, because I didn't know if I'd ever come home. By the time I started thinking about it, my mom told me you were with Earl. So...?" He shrugged and looked away again.

I could hardly compute. I'd been clinging to his perceived betrayal for so long, I didn't know what to think. I blurted out the first thing that came to mind. "You mean nothing happened with Shannon?"

His green gaze swung my way again, sending my stomach into another tailspin. Dear God. I was a mess on every possible level. My emotions were swirling like a tornado.

"Cade, I..." Flustered, my words sputtered.

His eyes softened, just the slightest bit.

"I know what you saw was bad, but I didn't even know she was there. She woke me up climbing in bed bare ass naked. That whole morning was a shitshow. You were gone, and I wake up to find fucking Shannon. Then you show up and storm out. Don't get me wrong, I understood why, but you didn't give me time to explain anything. When you wouldn't even talk to me for a whole damn week, I saw red and said fuck it. Took me three damn years to think maybe I should talk to you. By then, you were dating—hell, I don't know—someone. Time kept passing and then I heard you were engaged to Earl, so I figured it was best to let the past stay in the past."

Tears were hot in my eyes and I could hardly hear over the rushing sound in my ears. "Why, why would Shannon...?"

Cade shrugged. "Hell if I know. She was your friend." He started to say something else and stopped, swinging away to look out the window again.

After seven years of holding tight to my anger, I was struggling to let go. Strangely, I didn't doubt Cade. My anger, my pain and my frustration were all bundled together in a fist inside and looking for another target.

"How come you didn't try harder to talk to me?" I asked, feeling prickly all over.

After a few beats of silence while the space inside his truck became heavy, he spoke again. "Amelia, look we both blew this one. You had every right to be pissed off walking in on what you did. I knew I had nothing to do with Shannon's move, but I know how it looked. Maybe if I hadn't already been scheduled to leave so soon we could've kept from blowing things up so completely. By the time I calmed down, my life was in California and you were here. I meant to come back sooner, but then I heard you were with Earl and planning to get married. I, uh..." He paused to stare out the windshield again, his throat moving with a swallow.

"When the job opened up, I figured I'd come home. I missed it, so here I am."

"What job?" I asked, inanely focusing on the one detail that didn't hurt to think about.

Cade looked back at me, his gaze inscrutable again. "I took the foreman position with the hotshot crew in Willow Brook."

I nodded, but couldn't seem to think what to say next. Everything was all jumbled up inside. A teeny, tiny corner of my heart was doing cartwheels. I'd missed him so damn much for so long. To hear he was moving home was like the sun coming out after years in the dark. Yet, I'd worked so hard at shoving my feelings for him into a locked closet in a corner of my heart. I wasn't used to allowing myself to even think about those feelings, much less experience them.

"So, sounds like your wedding is off?" he asked, jumping tracks in our conversation.

We were traversing in such emotionally loaded territory, a linear track hardly made sense.

I nodded, wondering how much I'd said to him in my tipsy state last night.

"Yeah. I, uh, made a mess of it. Never should've said yes anyway."

"Why did you?"

Once upon a time, I'd loved how direct Cade was. At the moment, it was brutal. I wanted to bolt, and I couldn't. *You're no chicken, so don't start acting like one.* Thing was, Cade got to me. He was the only man who ever had. He made me feel vulnerable and off kilter. For crying out loud, I ran my own construction business—Kick A** Construction. I pushed against the uncertainty inside.

"I, uh... My answer sucks, but it is what it is. I figured it was the best chance I'd get."

At that, the tears I'd been fighting off flowed freely. I had to get the hell out of here. I fumbled with the door handle and stumbled out of his truck.

Chapter Six
CADE

"You saw Amelia?"

My mother's eyes were wide as she looked over at me from across the kitchen table. Georgia Masters was my tough as nails mother who hid behind a polite, friendly exterior. Her silver hair was shot through with a few lingering strands of dark brown. For many years, she'd left it long, but now it was short, the curls still a tad wild. I'd inherited my green eyes from her, along with the unruly brown hair. My mom was the town librarian—smart, friendly and as close to the town's nerve center as anyone was.

I took a gulp of the coffee she'd made for me and nodded. "Yup."

Mom leaned back in her chair. "Her mother is worried sick. Amelia ran, actually ran, out of the church and left Earl behind. Sarah said she hasn't returned her calls since she took off." She paused only to lean back and snatch her phone off the kitchen counter. "I'm calling Sarah. Where is Amelia now?"

I pondered what to say. I knew exactly where I'd left Amelia, but I didn't know whether she wanted anyone to know where she was. I might be wrestling with my resentments when it came to her, but I felt protective of her. She hadn't asked me to hide where she was, so I finally lifted a shoulder in a shrug. "Mom, I dunno if she wants anyone to know."

Mom narrowed her eyes, her lips thinning. "What happened?"

Her question didn't surprise me. In the years since I'd moved away, my mom had never stopped saying she wished I'd tried harder to talk to Amelia. She'd only shut up about it once Amelia got engaged to Earl. My mind spun back to the roughly twenty-four hours I'd spent with Amelia. After kissing her on the sidewalk in Anchorage, I'd spent the rest of the night mentally kicking myself for so easily falling prey to my desire. Yet, our past was what it was. Once upon a time, she'd meant the world to me. No woman even came close to what she meant. Not that I'd given anyone a chance to matter. I didn't think about it much, but I knew I might be perceived as cold. I eschewed attachments and made that crystal clear to any woman who crossed my path. A night between the sheets ended before I fell asleep. In fact, the other night with Amelia had been the first night I'd allowed myself to fall asleep with a woman since she'd walked out on me.

My heart clenched. Fuck. This was far more difficult than I'd anticipated. I'd figured on moving back to Willow Brook and learning to live with Amelia being married to someone else. I hadn't counted on what it would feel like to see her, and I certainly hadn't counted on her not being officially with someone else. Yesterday afternoon, she'd started crying and run out of my truck, the sight of her that upset nearly annihilating me. Even though I'd known she probably wanted to be left alone, fool that I was, I'd followed her out of the truck to the benches running along the railing at the viewing spot on the highway.

With a gorgeous view of Denali in the distance and a

river winding in a glittering ribbon through a field by the highway, I'd sat down beside her and waited. It had taken most of my discipline not to yank her into my arms, but I managed. Eventually, she'd wiped her face with the edge of my t-shirt—the one she'd been wearing—and looked over at me. Without a word, she'd stood, her eyes shuttered, and nodded. "I suppose we should get going."

I'd had so many things to say, but none of them seemed right. I hated, fucking hated, to hear she'd thought marrying Earl was the best chance she'd get. She had no idea—no fucking idea—how I would've given anything for a shot to clean up the mess between us. I had an idea why she thought that. I knew plenty of guys thought she was hot. Hell, I'd been in high school with most of them. Yet, she was a handful and intimidating as hell. Seeing as she stood eye to eye with most men at five-foot eleven and could hold her own just about anywhere, well, she wasn't easy. I'd been intimidated myself, but I'd wanted her so fiercely I hadn't let that stand in my way.

The flip side to her passionate, no-holds barred attitude—well, when she got mad, she got really mad. Just like she'd thrown her phone away after running out on Earl, she'd never once picked up my repeated calls to her in the days and weeks after she'd stormed out. Truth be told, I was so angry, I'd only tried a few times after I moved away if only to tell her off. Yesterday, I'd looked over at her and bit back my words. I needed time to get grounded in my own head before saying much more than I already had. So I'd driven the rest of the way to Willow Brook and dropped her off at her brother's cabin on the outskirts of town. There was no phone there, but she'd insisted she wanted to be left in peace, so I'd driven away. I'd made no promises to keep her whereabouts secret.

My mom cleared her throat, and I glanced up.

"Were you planning to answer my question?" she asked.

I took another gulp of coffee and considered what to say.

After a moment, I ran a hand through my hair with a sigh. "Mom, nothing happened."

She arched a brow. "I'm not stupid, Cade. I can tell by the look on your face something happened. Please tell me you two came to your senses and figured out you belong together."

"Mom, it's been seven years. Amelia just walked out on her fiancé yesterday. You can't seriously think I'd show up and everything would be sorted out that fast. I don't even know..."

"Don't even start with me," she snapped. "You two never got over each other. Good grief, Amelia was so determined not to talk about you, she'd walk out of the room if I even said your name at her mother's house. And you? You stayed in California six years longer than you planned just to avoid seeing that girl."

My mother's words were like a kick to the gut—the sickening kind. She was quite right, but I didn't like thinking about any of it. It stung to hear how hard Amelia worked not to hear the truth about what never happened with Shannon. She was as stubborn as me. If not more so.

My mom actually huffed before standing and snatching my empty coffee mug. She practically stomped to the counter and refilled it before returning. After a moment of silence, she looked back over at me. "Could you at least let me tell Sarah you ran into Amelia and she's okay?" she asked, referencing Amelia's mother.

"Yeah. If she's worried, tell her I dropped Amelia off at Quinn's cabin. I think Amelia wants a little peace and quiet before she has to face the music for running off right before her wedding. She didn't ask me to keep it quiet, so I figure her mom should know where she's at."

My mom eyed me for a long moment. Not for the first time, I wished she wasn't so damn perceptive. I could feel her trying to read into me. My heart and mind were one giant mess, and I sure as hell didn't want to try to make sense of it all with my mother. I loved her to pieces, and I knew I was blessed to have her as a mother, but a little privacy wouldn't hurt about now.

"Mom, don't stare me down, okay?"

She flashed a knowing smile. "You're just uncomfortable because I know you so well. Maybe you don't want to talk, but I will. I've said it before, so I'll say it again: don't let resentment keep you away from someone you love. Shannon stirred the pot and made an ugly mess for you and Amelia. Don't let her actions dictate your future. You finally have a chance to make things right with the only woman you ever loved. Do it."

At that, she took a slow sip of coffee and picked up her phone, standing to leave me at the table by myself.

"Sarah, it's me. Just talked to Cade and believe it or not, he gave Amelia a ride yesterday..."

My mother's words faded as she walked down the hallway. I savored another gulp of coffee and stared out the window. My parents' home was situated a few miles from downtown Willow Brook. They had a sprawling log home tucked into a cluster of cottonwood. This area of Alaska a mix of fields and rocky area as it was situated in the distant foothills of Denali, the famed centerpiece of the Alaska Range. The cottonwood opened up to a grassy field with a river running through it. I'd missed this view, missed it every day I'd been away.

Yet, I hadn't missed it as much as I'd missed Amelia.

Chapter Seven
AMELIA

I eyed the moose standing between my brother's battered truck and me. The moose in question, a gangly female yearling, stared back at me. Its brown fur looked soft, its dark eyes wide and curious. The moose looked so at ease, I might've been tempted to carry on and walk straight past it, but I knew better. Moose were near-sighted. I figured I looked like a blurry shape at this distance. If I were lucky, the moose would bolt in the opposite direction when I got close enough, but that was no guarantee. More people were injured by moose every year in Alaska than by bears. Moose weren't predatory, but they startled easy. You never knew if they'd run off or run at you, so it was best to steer clear.

I leaned against the deck railing and waited. A squirrel peered over at me from its perch on the railing a few feet away. I'd scattered sunflower seeds on the ground nearby this morning. The squirrel flicked its eyes from me to the ground before bursting into chatter and leaping to the ground. The chatter galvanized the moose yearling, and she jogged into the trees.

I gave it a few more minutes before stepping off the

porch and walking to Quinn's truck. My older brother Quinn was one of my favorite people. I figured he might be worried about me, but he'd give me the space I needed. His cabin was roughly a half hour outside of Willow Brook. He'd purchased it about a year ago when it came up for sale. He had no intention of living here, but he'd wanted a place nearby for when he visited with his wife Lacey. Only a few months ago, Lacey had given birth to their first daughter. They'd named her after our mother, Sarah. I adored Quinn and had been beyond happy when he finally saw the light of day and admitted he was in love with Lacey.

I couldn't help but wonder if Sarah's birth had been the trigger that snapped me out of my stupidity over Earl. I'd gone to Diamond Creek where Quinn and Lacey lived to meet baby Sarah. I'd left the next day wondering if I'd ever get lucky enough to find something like what they had. Quinn loved Lacey down to her bones—headstrong, willful, tomboy Lacey. I wanted someone to love me like that.

It wasn't that I hadn't known there wasn't much passion between Earl and me. I'd told Cade the truth when I said I thought Earl was the best chance I had. Because it had sure as hell seemed like it. Less than twenty-four hours with Cade had been a brutally painful reminder of what I'd once had.

I climbed into the beater truck Quinn had left parked here. Several attempts to get the engine to turn over failed. I leaned my head against the seat with a sigh. I hadn't been thinking clearly when I'd asked Cade to drop me off here yesterday. All I'd known was I needed to get the hell away from him before I did or said anything else stupid. I also hadn't been ready to face anyone in Willow Brook. Yet, here I was now with no phone and no way to go anywhere. Quinn and Lacey had plenty of food here, but I had quickly discovered being alone with my thoughts with next to nothing to distract me wasn't helping. At all.

I tossed and turned last night, my dreams a messy mix of fury and arousal. I'd woken in the midst of a heated dream, so hot it made me blush. Of course, the only man I ever dreamt about like that was Cade. Even worse, the dream was more vivid than any I'd had in years because I'd seen him. He'd gone from being a ghost of my past to a living, breathing raw manifestation of masculinity in the here and now.

With a muttered cruse, I leapt back out of the truck, only to find the curious yearling had returned and was nibbling on the bushes by the front porch. I put my hands on my hips and sighed. "Dammit! Moose, go find some food somewhere else," I called.

The yearling paused in its nibbling, its ear flicking in my direction for a second before it resumed eating. Another squirrel dashed past me on the stone walkway leading up to the cabin, racing to the scattered sunflower seeds and right under the feet of the yearling. I looked up at the cabin. It was a cute little place. The home was two stories in a perfect square with an angled roof to let the snow slide off in winter. Quinn had hired me to replace the roof last year, and I'd installed pretty blue steel roofing.

I glanced down at my t-shirt. I was still attired in Cade's t-shirt and the pair of jeans I'd grabbed at the department store by the hotel yesterday morning. With a sigh, I spun back to lean against the truck. The moose was happily chomping away on the bushes, so unless I felt inclined to chase it off, I'd have to wait it out.

I wished I hadn't been so stupid as to throw my phone away and, even worse, so stupid as to insist Cade drop me off here. I scanned the small clearing in front of the cabin, my eyes landing on the woodpile with an axe resting on the chopping stump. It was a good distance away from the moose. Fine. I'd chop some wood. It was the least I could do for Quinn and Lacey hosting me when they didn't even know I was here.

Chopping wood was so satisfying. Every swing of the axe, every thwack of it as it collided with the wood gave release to my pent up messy emotions. I must've been at it a good half hour when I heard the low rumble of an engine coming down the winding driveway. I'd finally managed to knock my mind off its loop of Cade, but it instantly swung back to him. No one else knew I was here.

With my pulse off to the races and my belly somersaulting, I looked over my shoulder to see his black truck rolling to a slow stop. I looked away and swung the axe again.

Chapter Eight
CADE

I walked across the gravel drive, my eyes on Amelia. She'd tied my too-big shirt in a knot at her waist, giving me a nice view of her lush bottom as she leaned forward to toss aside the wood she'd just split in two. She swung the axe again, efficiently splitting another log and promptly moving onto the next. When I reached her side, she stopped, letting the axe fall to the ground. She dragged her sleeve across her face and looked over at me. Her hair was loose and fell in honey-brown waves around her shoulders. Her skin was flushed and her eyes uncertain.

Just like that, I was hard. Fuck. Amelia made me crazy. I didn't even know why I was here. All I knew was I got worried about her mom heading out this way once she found out where Amelia was. The second I started worrying about that, I was calling out to my mom I'd be back later and taking off.

I tore my eyes from hers—the amber-gold gaze that grabbed at me—and scanned the yard. A yearling stood by the porch basically destroying the bushes there, and a few squirrels were busy running back and forth. I managed a breath and tried to talk my body down. Another breath, and I thought I could look at her again.

She stood there, one hand on her hip, and all I wanted was to lift her into my arms and find somewhere to lose myself in her. I recalled my mother's comments about us and about me finally getting a chance to make things right. If only it were that easy.

I swatted those thoughts aside and eyed Amelia. "Thought I'd drop by. You didn't ask me not to tell anyone where you were. My mom hounded me about at least letting your mom know you're okay, so I caved. If I should've kept my mouth shut, I'm sorry. Thought you might want to know."

Amelia was quiet and then nodded slowly. "Right. I didn't expect you to keep it a secret. I, uh, well, I guess I realized it wasn't the brightest idea to be out here without a phone. Quinn's truck won't start," she said, gesturing toward an old truck that had definitely seen better days.

I glanced to the truck and back to her. "Don't imagine it would. Looks like it's been sitting in one place for most of the year," I said, pointing to the tires settled into the ground.

"Maybe you can give it a jump," Amelia said, her voice lilting slightly in question.

I was instantly disappointed. Not because of what she said specifically, but because of what it meant. If the truck started up, I'd be expected to leave as soon as it did. While I couldn't have said precisely why I was here, I sure as hell didn't want to leave. *Yeah, and it's gonna look great for you to refuse to help with the truck. Man up and help her out.*

I was nodding before I realized it. Since talking didn't make a lick of sense with us, I simply walked back to my truck. In short order, I had it parked in front of the old truck and was hooking up the jumper cables. A few tries and nothing happened. Amelia climbed out of Quinn's truck and came to stare under the hood.

"Are you sure you hooked it up right?" she asked, glancing from the truck battery to me.

I didn't even try not to roll my eyes. "Seriously, Lia?" I swung a palm across the span between the two trucks. "Feel free to check."

Amelia's eyes went wide and her nostrils flared. I abruptly realized I'd just called her by my old nickname for her. Most of the time, I called her Amelia like everyone else did. But when we were alone, sometimes I called her Lia. I felt as if I'd just been kicked in the chest—it hurt that much to remember.

She didn't say a word and finally tore her gaze free, her eyes traveling along the jumper cables from my truck battery to the other one. "Of course you got it right," she said softly. She looked up again, her eyes shuttered. "Let's try one more time. Okay?"

Another attempt to no avail. Amelia climbed back out of Quinn's old truck and unhooked the jumper cables, carefully coiling them before handing them back to me. My fingers brushed hers when I took them, sending a hot jolt of electricity straight through me. I returned them to my truck and closed the hood. I glanced back to the cabin and chuckled.

"Hope Quinn wasn't too attached to those bushes," I offered as I watched the yearling nibble one down.

Amelia followed my gaze and laughed softly. "Lacey probably won't be too thrilled. She planted those last summer."

"Lacey?"

She looked to me, her eyes puzzled. After a second, the confusion cleared. "Oh right. You probably missed the fact Quinn got married. After he finished med school and his overseas jaunts, he came home. He took a position at a medical clinic in Diamond Creek. Well, it's more than a position. He's taking over the whole clinic from the doctor retiring there. I don't know if you ever met Lacey, but they were friends for years. She used to do those backcountry trips with him. Anyway, they finally got a clue and realized they were perfect for each other. Quinn bought this cabin about a year ago so they'd have a place to stay when they came up to visit mom and me."

It occurred to me I'd missed a lot of details about friends and family in Willow Brook. I hadn't had to try too hard. Life as a hotshot firefighter didn't leave a ton of time to visit. It bothered me to realize I felt as if there was a giant hole in my understanding of Amelia—I'd missed so much time. I beat back my regrets and looked over at her. "Good for Quinn. I think I remember Lacey. She came to visit a few times—hard-core hiker, right?"

Amelia laughed. "That's one way to describe her. She runs her own guiding business. Quinn helps out a little, but she's backed off handling most of the trips. She's got MS and now they have the baby. If you're here to stay, I'm sure you'll see them around town. They come up every few months."

I nodded and figured maybe we could have a normal conversation. That's all we needed—a little practice acting normal and maybe I'd stop feeling so crazy around her.

"It'd be good to see Quinn. Haven't seen him in years," I finally said, realizing as soon as the words left my mouth, everything circled back to Amelia and our ugly break up.

I hadn't seen Quinn in years because I'd mostly avoided Willow Brook for all of the last seven years. The only thing that got me home was my parents, and I'd kept those visits brief. Silence fell between us again. I scanned the yard, my eyes circling around until I noticed another moose walking down the driveway.

"We've got more company."

Amelia followed my gaze and looked back to me with a sigh. "You can tell no one's around much. I'm guessing they think we're in their territory, which I suppose we are."

She bit her lip, worrying it with her teeth, and blood shot straight to my groin. Hell. She needed to stop doing that. *Man, for you to get a grip, she'd have to stop existing.* So true and I damn well knew it.

Another glance down the driveway, and I saw our latest visitor was a full-grown bull moose. It wasn't mating season yet when the bull moose would be at their boldest, but it wouldn't be wise to stay where we were.

"Come on," I said, slipping my hand around Amelia's. "Let's get inside. We've got a better shot at getting past our young buddy over there than playing chicken with this guy."

Amelia moved at my side without hesitation, her stride long and sure. "Hey moose, we're coming by!" she called out as we approached the yearling.

The yearling's head whipped up. However, it remained in place as we passed by. Amelia never let go of my hand as she opened the door, and we stepped inside the cabin. I didn't think I could let go. Not just yet. Just the simple feel of her hand held in mine felt so damn good, my pulse was thundering.

I scanned the room we entered. Light fell through the windows on the far wall, which looked out through the spruce trees to a secluded lake. The space was airy and open with a couch and two rocking chairs situated near a woodstove on the back wall. A kitchen with copper pots and pans hanging from a decorative rack was to one side with a low curved island serving as seating. A spiral staircase led upstairs to where I presumed there were bedrooms since the only door down here was to the side of the kitchen.

I glanced to Amelia who hadn't moved since she'd closed the door behind us. The sun splashing into the room caught in her hair, gilding it with gold. She didn't even have to try, and I wanted her so fiercely, I could hardly contain the need pounding through me. Seven fucking years, and she still had me in her grip. I'd been so damn foolish to think I could come home and keep my distance.

She stared at me, her honey-amber gaze darkening to cognac. I knew what I saw in her eyes. I could only hope she wanted me as desperately as I wanted her.

My sanity was washed away in the roaring current of

need—pure, raw lust was what it was. Her hand was warm in mine. I turned to face her, stroking my thumb in slow passes over her wrist where I could feel her pulse racing. I stepped closer until I was almost flush against her. Her breasts rose and fell against my chest with her ragged breathing. I took a grim satisfaction in knowing she might be as far gone as I was.

I felt driven—driven by years of missing her, by years of empty sex with women who meant next to nothing, and by years of anger and resentment at what we'd lost and to nothing but someone else's lies. I hung on to the thinnest thread of control as I stood there, my cock hard and my body nearly a slave to my need for her. After a few beats, I took another step, crowding against her. I could feel the fine shudder running through her body.

Her skin was still flushed, and her hair a tousled mess from chopping wood. Raw need lashed at me. I told myself I couldn't let things go too far. Not right now. But I wouldn't forgo a taste of what I wanted so desperately.

She backed away, and I followed. Only a few steps, and her hips bumped into the counter. I freed her hand and slid both of mine roughly down her sides to curl around her hips and lift her onto the counter.

"Cade."

She said my name as if it were a plea—rough and raspy.

"Lia."

Her name came out rough and harsh, weighted with years of need, longing, anger and regret.

I tugged her hips to the edge of the counter and stepped between her knees. I might be half out of my mind, but I needed to give her a chance to tell me to back the hell off.

"Tell me you don't want this," I murmured.

Her flush deepened. She shook her head. "I can't."

"What *do* you want?"

She swallowed as my hands slid over the curves of her

hips and up her sides. I palmed one of her breasts, savoring its lush, heavy weight.

She hadn't answered me yet. I dragged my thumb back and forth across her nipple, taut and erect through my t-shirt. "You're not answering me."

I didn't know who I was right now. We'd always been a bit wild when it came to sex—riding the rough edge. Amelia was such a force in everything and sex was no exception. With us, it was like match after match after match to the flames between us. Yet, even with the memory of what it had been like with her, I was teetering on a dangerous edge now. With a tumult of emotions lashing at me, I was at the edge of my restraint. I had to know she was as wrecked as I was.

Still toying with her nipple with one hand, I slipped the other up around her neck, lacing it into her tousled hair. My thumb brushed over the wild beat of her pulse. "Lia...come on. Don't hide from me."

"I want you," she finally said, her eyes flashing with need and something else.

"It's just like I said when you found me. I might've been drunk and a mess, but it was the truth. It's always been you. No one else. To everyone else, I'm too..." She stopped, anger flashing in her eyes.

I couldn't help it and arched into her, almost groaning at the feel of her heated core. She murmured something and then tilted her eyes up. I thought she meant to say something. Instead, she yanked me to her, our mouths colliding in a fierce kiss.

Chapter Nine
AMELIA

I tumbled into the madness of Cade's kiss. He'd always been a good kisser—a mix of rough and tender—but he was a damn master at it now. Deep sweeps of his tongue against mine, nibbles on my lower lip, slow traces of my lips—hot, wet and overpowering. My senses were obliterated to the point I didn't even notice when he yanked the t-shirt over my head. Hell, I hadn't realized I'd already shoved his shirt off until he stepped closer, and I groaned at the feel of his hard muscled chest against me. His skin was hot and smooth. I wouldn't have thought it possible for him to have gotten more fit since I'd known him before, but either my memory failed me, or he had. He was hard muscle all over, and I couldn't get enough. I so often felt too large, too tall and ungainly around other men. I never felt like that with Cade.

Cade was actually taller than me, but it wasn't that. Somehow, he made me feel encompassed in his embrace whenever I was with him. I certainly didn't need any protecting, but I felt protected when I was with him—as if he'd fend anything off. The feeling gave me an odd sense of freedom, as if I could let go in a way I didn't usually. The feeling was so rare, I collapsed into it and let myself be swept into the madness that existed only with him.

His lips blazed a wet trail of fire down along my neck, while I mapped his chest with my hands, savoring every hard planed muscle. I cried out when he yanked my bra off and closed his warm mouth over a nipple. I almost came from that alone. I hadn't had an orgasm with anything other than my vibrator for seven years, along with everything else that went with the bitterness of our break up. All I wanted was him. Now.

I dragged my hand over the bulge of his cock, savoring his rough groan against my skin. He lifted his head, his dark green gaze locking with mine. He'd already torn the buttons of my jeans open and teased me mercilessly by dragging his fingers back and forth over the denim, but now he hooked a finger over the edge of my underwear and sifted down through my curls, straight into my drenched folds.

I didn't even bother to hide my groan. I was so far gone, I didn't care.

Cade's forehead fell to mine, his lips a whisper away. "You're so wet," he murmured.

My only response was a moan when he dragged his thumb across my clit—just once and just enough to make me nearly lose it. He sank a finger into me, driving deep. I cried out, my hips rolling into his touch. Another finger joined the first and he toyed with me, spreading and teasing me, his thumb flitting across my clit.

I chased after my release, but he held me back, bringing me to the precipice and then pulling back. Nearly wild with need and desperate, I swore.

"Cade, if you don't..."

He chuckled. "That's my girl. I love it when you get mad."

That did it. I slipped my hand into his briefs, sighing at the hot velvety skin over his hard cock. His breath hissed and he stopped teasing me. He drove into me deeply, fucking me with his fingers and sending me spinning in a burst of sharp pleasure.

Chapter Ten
CADE

I stared down at Amelia, my heart tightening amidst its thunderous beat. Damn. Amelia was glorious when she let go. Her throaty cry was music to my body, strumming every fiber. She sat before me on the counter, her long legs curled around my hips, her cheeks flushed, and her lips swollen. Her channel clenched around my fingers, its pulses slowing. My gaze dipped down to her breasts—full and lush, her nipples damp and dusky pink. I hadn't forgotten any of her, yet everything had faded. The sharpness of now pierced me straight through the heart. All of her—how she looked, how she felt, the way we felt together—was blinding in its shimmering brightness, and I could barely catch my breath.

She sighed, her legs relaxing around my hips. I managed to drag my eyes up to find hers waiting. Before I had a chance to form a thought, she was shoving my jeans down around my hips, and my cock bounced free. Amelia pushed me back swiftly as she shimmied her hips off the counter. Her hand stroked me lightly before she dragged her tongue up one side and down the other. My knees almost gave out when she looked up. Her lashes were glinted with gold from the sun angling through the windows, framing her eyes dark with desire and a hint of mischief there. She loved having me at her mercy and knew quite well she had me there now with my cock in her fist and her lips a mere inch away.

She waited a beat—her eyes locked to mine—and then dipped her head, swirling her tongue around the end of my cock and drawing me into her mouth. I'd have liked to think I had more control. Hell, I was way past being young and quick. But I'd gone seven long years without the one and only woman who could slay me—body, heart and soul. Her warm mouth around me—her tongue and lips making naughty with me—and I was so close to release, I gritted my teeth. Another slow drag of her tongue along the underside of my cock before she drew me in again, and that was it. My release thundered through me.

Amelia slowly drew back, not batting an eye at the fact I'd just spent myself in her mouth. She'd never been a prude before and wasn't now. She straightened and leaned her hips on the counter. Somewhere in the midst of my roaring release, I'd rested my hands on the counter behind her, leaving her standing in the cage of my arms. My breath heaved a few more times as I tried to get back to some place of control. I finally straightened and met her eyes. The corner of her mouth curled in a smile, her cheeks pinkening slightly.

Watching her, I wrestled with what I wanted—to lift her in my arms and cart her upstairs to where I figured there must be a bed. Taking that step seemed almost dangerous—too intimate, too much of what I wanted, too much of everything I wasn't sure I could have. Not until we took the time to untangle the mess of regret and misunderstanding between us. It was one thing to state the facts of what happened—a well-timed fabrication sent us spinning away from each other—and yet another thing to get through to the other side of the emotional mess between us with years apart layered on top of it.

We stood like that for several minutes. Amelia's half-smile faded, and she started to look anxious. She masked it well, but I knew her probably better than I knew myself. I shook my head. "Don't."

"Don't what?" she countered.

"Don't go wherever it is you're going in your head. I didn't mean to, well, let things get out of hand, but it's not like we don't both know what's right here between us."

She was quiet and finally nodded. It should have felt awkward—hell, we'd just about lost ourselves in each other —but it didn't. I tried to recall the last time I hadn't practically raced away from a woman I'd been skin to skin with and couldn't recall a single one...except for Amelia.

I stepped back, trailing my fingers along her arm, a subtle buzz of satisfaction rolling through me when I felt her skin pebble under my touch. I forced myself to take another step back and leaned down to snag her shirt off the floor. Rather, it was my shirt, but she was wearing it. I gained an odd sense of satisfaction to know she'd been wearing my clothes.

After she'd hidden her way too tempting breasts behind her bra and my shirt and I'd buttoned my jeans, she rounded the low counter and glanced over her shoulder. "Coffee? Or something else?"

I stared at her and found myself nodding because I didn't know what else to do. What was the usual thing to do when I'd missed her fiercely for seven years, when I had plenty of resentment at the way she'd shut me out without a chance to set the story straight, and when I'd finally been able to give into what I'd missed almost as much as I'd miss air if I couldn't breathe?

Well, it seemed the mundane was the best option, so coffee it was. I hooked my boot over the rung of a stool and tugged it away from the counter. Sliding onto it, I leaned on an elbow and watched her start the coffee.

Chapter Eleven
AMELIA

I stepped to the ground and carefully brought the extension ladder down from the roof. I was finishing up a roof replacement project today. I'd hitched a ride back to town with Cade after he'd stopped by and proceeded to remind me so very thoroughly of why I'd never gotten over him. I'd called my mom to let her know I was back. My mom had been restrained with her questions for me, but I knew she had to be worried, seeing as I'd walked out on my wedding. I figured I'd have to barrel through the gossip I'd created by dumping Earl. Work gave me something to do. Aside from that, I could barely stop obsessing about Cade, so I needed something to keep me busy.

I glanced over to see Lucy Caldwell leaning against our work truck. Lucy with her blonde hair, blue eyes and curvy figure that she hid effectively in her heavy duty construction gear. Lucy was kind enough to not pester me with questions when I said I'd be meeting her at the job site today. Lucy was my sole full-time employee in the small construction company I started about five years ago. Kick A** Construction was its name—one I'd chosen as a play on the common bumper stickers in Alaska bearing the phrase *Alaskan Girls Kick Ass*.

I had always loved working outside and loved to build. When I was little, my very first project had been a doghouse for the family dog, Dora. It had been lopsided, and my mother and Quinn had helped right it, but it had been the most fun I'd ever had. As life rolled along, I kept taking on little projects here and there. I went to college in Anchorage, heavy in the middle of my heady love with Cade, and majored in architecture. After everything blew up with Cade, I'd been at loose ends. At the time, we'd recently moved back to Willow Brook. I'd taken a job at the Firehouse Café, a local coffee shop and restaurant, and had been casting about for what to do. Cade had been scheduled to leave for a full year of training to become a hotshot firefighter in California. We'd talked about whether I might move with him, but money had been tight at the time.

It had never occurred to me our relationship might blow apart. He'd taken that flight to California, and I'd been so damn angry, I could hardly see straight. In between shifts at the café, I started picking up odd jobs as a contractor. Before I knew it, I was doing that full-time and had to make some choices about making my business official. Kick A** Construction was formed. At first, it had been just me. My small jobs led to recommendations for bigger jobs, and I needed help. I'd known Lucy in passing then. Lucy had moved to Alaska when we were in high school, a point when my circle of friends had been pretty set. Shannon, my once upon a time friend who betrayed me so horribly, had blown that circle to smithereens.

Lucy overheard me worrying about how many jobs I could do at the café one day and offered to help. We made a kick ass team.

I gave her a wave and hooked the ladder under my arm, walking across the yard to heft it atop the truck. Without a word, Lucy reached up to help me guide it on the racks and adjust the fittings to hold it in place.

We leaned against the tailgate. I surveyed the new roof we'd installed on the small home. "Looks good."

Lucy giggled. "Roofs don't need to look good, although this one does if only because it's red. Roofs are like shoes. You need them. They're practical, but they don't need to be pretty."

I looked to Lucy and shook my head. "Can't I enjoy the fact it's pretty? I mean, the red looks nice in the trees," I said, gesturing toward the red steel roof.

Lucy rolled her eyes. "Of course you can enjoy it. Just pointing out that it's a roof. It needs to keep the elements out." She glanced down at her watch and brushed a streak of dirt off her arm. "It's only noon. Should we head over to get started at the Jacobson's job or wait until tomorrow?"

We were scheduled to start a new house project this week. I eyed Lucy, considering her question. "Let's start tomorrow. I'd like to take another look at the drawings and stop by Denali Builders to make sure all of our orders are lined up."

Lucy nodded. "Sounds good. Wanna grab some lunch first?"

"Sure. Firehouse?"

At Lucy's nod, we climbed into the truck. A short drive into downtown and I rolled into a parking spot in front of Firehouse Café. Downtown Willow Brook was picturesque, situated in a valley in the foothills of the Alaska Range with Swan Lake in view. The lake was fed from several streams rolling downhill from the distant mountains and offered a gorgeous view in all seasons. The lake was the entire reason Willow Brook was founded. It offered fresh water and fishing all summer long. The town's convenience to Anchorage allowed residents to enjoy the benefits of living in a small, wilder area, yet the ability to run to Anchorage within a day for errands. Tourists passed through and kept local businesses quite busy from spring through autumn, yet the town retained its small feel with only a core group of year-round residents.

I climbed out of the truck and glanced around. Firehouse Café was on Main Street. It was actually housed in the town's old fire station. It was a tall square building with the old garage turned into a seating area for dining and an open style bakery and kitchen. The fire poles were painted brightly with fireweed flowers, the finishing touches on the bright colors throughout the café with the window frames in a variety of colors and artwork hung on the walls. Square wooden tables were scattered about for seating with a counter offering additional seating where customers had a clear view into the kitchen and bakery. The bright colors livened up the long, dark winters.

No matter the season, Firehouse Café was busy. Lucy spied a table opening up in the corner and dashed across the restaurant to snag it. She grinned widely when I caught up and slipped into the chair across from her. "Hope you didn't trip anyone else on the way to the table," I commented with a shake of my head.

Lucy giggled and reached up to adjust her ponytail. If you overlooked her clothes—usually battered jeans and t-shirts and hardly ever feminine—you might think she was fragile. With her blonde hair, bright blue eyes and creamy complexion, she was beautiful. She had a girly giggle and was on the short side. Yet, she was as tomboy as anyone I'd ever known. She ignored her looks and didn't do a thing to show them off. She was a damn hard worker and never flinched at getting dirty or swinging a hammer all day long. I loved working with her and felt lucky Lucy had overheard my conversation that day. Lucy had become my best friend too. Seeing as we spent a ton of time together, that was a major bonus.

"Hey girls! Two coffees?" Janet James asked as she passed

our table with a tray full of dirty dishes. Janet was the owner of the café and was there almost all the time.

"You got it," I said quickly.

"Give me a few," Janet said as she walked swiftly to the counter and slipped behind it, disappearing through a swinging door.

A line cook was busy at the grill, swiftly sliding food onto plates, which were whisked away by the waitress. I scanned the café, a bit relieved I didn't see anyone I knew too well. Oh, I knew most everyone at a glance, but I'd been laying low in the days since I'd come back on the heels of my disastrous wedding that never was. Lucy took a call on her phone, and my mind instantly skipped to Cade. This was becoming a problem. If I didn't have something to do or someone to talk to, Cade strolled into my thoughts—bold as ever.

Only two days had passed since I'd almost lost my mind over him, and I'd wasted countless hours thinking about him. All I wanted was to see him again...and again and again. Somehow, we'd gotten to a place of sort of normal before he'd offered me a ride back to Willow Brook. I'd wanted—desperately wanted—to hide away at Quinn's cabin with Cade and just forget about everything else. But it wasn't that simple, and I damn well knew it. He might've brought me to the only orgasm I'd had with someone else in seven years, but that didn't mean we'd managed to wade through the all the hurt from before.

I was still trying to absorb what he'd told me on the drive back from Anchorage. I definitely got that he'd been hurt and angry I never even gave him a chance to explain. I'd been too damn angry to see him and talk to him. I'd shied away from thinking about any of it for most of the time. It hurt too much. Thinking about it now, I was tempted to start asking anyone who might know more about how stupid I'd been. Shannon had never once tried to talk to me before she moved away. I knew there would be a few people who might have the lowdown on why Shannon did what she did.

"Yoohoo, you're zoning out again," Lucy said, waving her hand back and forth.

I looked up from the table. "Huh?"

Lucy rolled her eyes. "Okay. Time to chat," she said matter-of-factly. "You walked out on Earl. I'm not gonna say…"

"Oh, you can tell me you told me so. You did," I said with a sad smile. Lucy had shared her concern more than once that Earl and I were, well, Lucy's description for it was 'like bland oatmeal.'

Lucy smiled, but it didn't reach her eyes. "I don't want to tell you I told you so because I wish I'd been wrong. I've left you be since you showed up out of nowhere for work yesterday, but mind telling me how you're doing?"

I shrugged and rolled my hand back and forth. "Not great. I feel like shit. I decided I should at least face Earl right off when I got back to town the day before yesterday, but he wasn't home."

Lucy leaned back in her chair when Janet approached our table. She set two coffees down and glanced between us. "Food?"

"Just bring us the lunch special today," Lucy said.

"Two salmon burgers. Anything with them?" Janet returned.

"Fries," I added.

"Got it," Janet called as she spun away.

Lucy took a sip of her coffee and angled her head to the side. "Earl's not home because he took off on a fishing trip with his brother." She didn't succeed in masking the slight curl to her lip.

Lucy had been pretty direct that she didn't think Earl appreciated me for who I was. She hadn't known me well when I'd been with Cade, so she hadn't known how much I knew I was missing.

I stared at her. "He went on a fishing trip?"

Lucy sighed. "Uh huh. Amelia, I'd like to say the guy was

crushed when you left him before he even got to the altar, but he wasn't. He told his dad what happened, and they came out together to announce the wedding was off. While we were all wondering where the hell you were and your mom was freaking out, he told everyone to enjoy the reception next door. Next thing I heard, he'd left to go fishing with Dan." Lucy ended with a shrug, her eyes scanning my face.

I felt the sting in my heart. It would be flat ridiculous for me to feel heartbroken over learning my ex-fiancé had so easily accepted me walking out on our wedding. It hurt only in the sense that it reinforced all the reasons I'd bolted. If there was one question I'd like to ask Earl—when he returned from his flipping fishing trip—it would be what he'd wanted from being with me in the first place.

"You okay?" Lucy asked.

I took a gulp of my coffee. "I'm fine. It just sucks. It's exactly why I couldn't go through with marrying him. I wish like hell I'd come to my senses a lot sooner, but it is what it is." I paused and glanced to the door when I heard the bells jingle its opening.

A cluster of hikers entered. I couldn't help but feel a tiny bit disappointed. I kept expecting to see Cade and beating back the hope every time I didn't.

"Okay, something else is up with you? I guess I figured the whole wedding-not wedding would be what's on your mind, but that's not it," Lucy said, her eyes narrowing when I glanced back her way.

I couldn't hide the flush that heated my cheeks. Lucy didn't say another word and angled her head to the side.

I took another gulp of coffee, nearly slamming my mug down on the table.

"Fine. I saw Cade."

"Cade Masters? The guy you were gaga over before. I barely knew him in high school, but it was impossible not to know who he was. All the girls drooled over him. I know about the whole ugly mess with your old friend Shannon. So what happened?"

I closed my eyes and took a breath. "He happened to show up at the bar where I might've gotten in a fistfight," I said, gesturing to my fading black eye.

Fortunately, the guy who'd punched me had shitty aim. He'd connected with my face, but his fist had slid off of my cheek after a glancing blow. The bruising wasn't too bad and already fading.

Lucy's eyes widened. "You know, I should win some serious points for keeping my mouth shut on that. I took one look at you and knew there was a story, but I figured you'd tell me in good time. You started a fight, got a black eye and your old boyfriend showed up to rescue you?"

"That about sums it up."

Lucy circled her hand in the air. "Oh, you're not even close to done. What else happened?"

My mind flashed to the hot, mind-bending, heart-clenching moments at the cabin. Just thinking about it sent heat sliding through my veins. I looked over at Lucy and sighed. "Maybe a little bit more. I'm all mixed up," I said, my voice cracking at the end.

The teasing gleam disappeared from Lucy's eyes. "Hey, it's okay. It's been a bumpy few days for you. I didn't mean..." She paused when Janet arrived to serve our food.

I was relieved at the interruption. I was also beyond grateful Lucy was the kind of friend she was. Lucy intuitively knew when someone needed space and didn't mind giving it to them. She settled in to eat, while I nibbled at my food, too mentally distracted to do much of anything else. I'd worked so hard at shoving thoughts of Cade out of my mind for so long, it was hard to think about him, much less talk about him. He'd occupied a huge place in my heart once upon a time. Then, it shattered into pieces. I'd avoided the shards of glass by sweeping them out of sight. In a few short days, I'd averted making a huge mistake by walking out on

Earl, seen Cade for the first time in too long, and learned that my version of his betrayal was a bit off. I knew he harbored his own pain and resentment. I could feel it radiating from him. There was a jumble of tangled emotions to get through, and I didn't even know how to talk about him.

After a few minutes of eating, I looked over at Lucy. "Me and Cade are messy. I loved him like crazy and then it all blew up. We had a chance to talk and, well, it seems like maybe I missed a few details of how things went down with Shannon."

Lucy paused in her chewing and took a giant gulp of water from the glass Janet had set on the table beside her. "Wait a minute. You never talk about Cade. Like ever. I left it alone because I figured, well, it was the past. What did you miss? Please tell me you knew he never had anything to do with Shannon. Because even I knew that."

My mouth fell open. "Huh? How do you know that?"

Lucy smacked her forehead with her hand. "Everyone knows. Just like everyone knows talking about Cade around you means you walk away. Okay, I wasn't close to you back then, so better to hear it from me than anyone else. Shannon had a nasty breakup, remember? I don't even know the guy's name, but some guy from college."

I nodded, my gut churning. It was making me sick to realize maybe I'd made things worse by being so damn determined not to talk about Cade.

Lucy continued, "Anyway, she came back to town and made a play for Cade right away. He threw her out and that was that. Trust me, ask anyone. Shannon was all pissy about the whole thing." Lucy paused for another bite of her burger. After she finished chewing, she looked over at me. "Do you mean to tell me you're so damn stubborn, you never figured this out?"

I swallowed against the tightness in my chest and nodded. That was me all right, stubborn as hell.

Lucy's eyes got sad. "Oh hon. Good grief. That sucks. I

mean, all anyone ever says about you and Cade was you two were perfect together. So what happened when you saw him? How do you feel?"

The bell over the door jingled again, and I reflexively glanced over my shoulder. Cade strode in, his subtle, almost lazy swagger making me hot all over. His brown hair was mussed. With him attired in faded black jeans that hugged his muscled legs and a black t-shirt that did absolutely nothing to disguise every inch of his hard chest, all I could do was stare at him.

His eyes caught mine from across the room, and he angled his head slightly in recognition. My pulse lunged, butterflies amassed in my belly, and my mouth went dry.

"Oh God," Lucy said wryly.

I tore my eyes from Cade and looked over at Lucy. "What?"

Lucy's mouth curled up at once corner as she shook her head slowly. "Well, now I know why Earl never did a thing for you. Girl, you have got it bad and so does he. Be careful and don't burn this place down just looking at each other."

Chapter Twelve

CADE

I forced my feet in the direction of the counter, but damn, I had to make myself walk that way. I knew Amelia was here the second I stepped through the door. I could feel her before I looked over and saw her. I made it to the counter and glanced at the chalkboard mounted on the wall by the cash register. Firehouse Café was an old favorite of mine, well of anyone in town really. Janet served good food and kept the place lively. It didn't hurt she'd been born and raised in Willow Brook, so she knew pretty much everyone and would help anyone in need. In the seven years I'd been gone, I hadn't set foot in here a single time during my visits home. It reminded me too much of Amelia. For starters, she'd worked here off and on, but we'd also spent plenty of time here grabbing coffee or food together.

Two line cooks were busy at the grill with customers filling the stools at the counter. Being mid-summer, there were plenty of unfamiliar faces here, along with a mix of locals. The swinging door into the back opened, and Janet stepped through, her face stretching in a wide smile the moment she laid eyes on me.

"Cade Masters! I was wondering when you'd stop in. I heard from your mama you were back for good," Janet said as she rounded the counter and pulled me into a hug.

I chuckled when she stepped back and pinched my cheek. Even my own mother didn't do that anymore, but Janet could get away with it. "You look as handsome as ever. How are you?" she asked, her brown eyes crinkling at the corners with her smile.

The last time I'd seen her, her hair had a few streaks of silver. Now it was mostly silver with streaks of dark brown. She gave off a warm, motherly air, reinforced with her round figure and face, yet that air hid a spine of steel. She'd run this café on her own for years after her first husband died in a car accident on an icy highway up north.

I grinned back at her. "I'm doing all right. It's good to see you. Really good."

Janet glanced over her shoulder to reply to something one of the line cooks had said and then turned back. "Let me get you something to eat and drink. It's on me today. What'll you have?"

"Start me off with some coffee." I paused and glanced around the café. Not a single table was open and the counter was packed. "Guess I'll wait to find somewhere to sit."

When I met Janet's eyes again, she arched a brow and barely nudged her chin in Amelia's direction. "You could join Amelia and Lucy. I'm sure they won't mind," she said with a gleam in her eyes.

I chuckled. "Not so sure about that."

Janet put her hand on her hip and leveled me with a glare. "I know you gave her a ride back to Willow Brook, so no sense in playing dumb with me. Don't worry about the gossip. She and Earl never should've been together. He thought she was some kind of challenge he could win. That man never appreciated her for who she was and isn't the least bit heartbroken over her walking out on their wedding. Oh, maybe his pride took a hit, but nothing more. You go talk to that girl. If you mean to set things right, you can't tiptoe around it."

I opened my mouth and then snapped it shut. Janet laughed softly and spun around to get me a coffee. When she handed it back, she winked. "Plus, there's nowhere else to sit anyway."

I simply shook my head, but damn if I didn't find myself doing just what she said. Janet had that effect on people—they tended to listen to her. I threaded through the tables on the way to the corner where Amelia sat with Lucy Caldwell. I knew Lucy in passing, but not too well. She'd moved to Willow Brook sometime when we were all in high school. She'd certainly turned heads for the guys with her blonde-haired, blue-eyed beauty, but she'd been entirely uninterested in any of them. I'd done a little reconnaissance about Amelia in the few days since she'd grabbed ahold of my heart and body again after our way too brief encounter at her brother's cabin. Well, truth be told, all I'd had to do was drop a few hints with my mom, and she opened the floodgates about Amelia. It was obvious she'd been holding back to the point she was almost resentful with me about it.

She'd told me Amelia had dated here and there and only seemed to get serious with Earl a year or two ago. Apparently, Amelia owned her own construction business now and Lucy worked with her. According to my mother, she hired out a few other contractors here and there, but Lucy was her only full-time employee.

Back when I'd been setting things up to do my training as a hotshot firefighter, she'd seemed at loose ends. I loved knowing she'd ended up doing something she enjoyed and was damn good at. I knew well it likely wouldn't work out too great for her to try to sign onto another crew. Not many women worked in the construction and contracting field. Not even in Alaska where women swapped back and forth between being just as feminine as anywhere you'd find and then hiking mountains and hunting and fishing with the best of men. Amelia also had a rather strong independent streak. She liked to do things on her own terms. The flip side was when she got angry, she let it drive her too far sometimes. I had enough sense to know that part of her had certainly contributed to how thoroughly she'd shut me out.

I stepped around a backpack strewn on the floor and reached the table where Amelia and Lucy were seated. Lucy glanced up first, her blue eyes round and heavily lashed with thick blonde eyelashes. She didn't do a thing for me, but I could imagine she drove the guys here crazy. Her looks were quite the contrast to her attire with her battered jeans, loose t-shirt, and a streak of dirt on her arm. "Hi Cade," she said brightly. "I'm not sure you remember me."

I inclined my head. "Lucy Caldwell. I might not have known you well, but I remember you."

Lucy's grin widened. "Good to know. How about you join us?"

I glanced to Amelia who'd lifted her gaze to me. Her cheeks were flushed. If she thought otherwise, she didn't say a word at Lucy's invitation. I could feel the turmoil rolling off of her in waves. I didn't give a damn. I'd felt tossed adrift on a rocky shore after she iced me out of her life, and I knew perfectly well we had something not many people ever had a shot at. I wasn't letting another chance slide by, no matter how much I was wrestling with my own tangled emotions.

I hooked my hand over the back of the chair and slipped into it. "Thanks for letting me join you," I said, smiling slightly at Lucy before looking directly at Amelia.

With Lucy and Amelia facing each other, I was seated between them. Amelia lifted her chin slightly, and I fought the urge to lean over and kiss her. I had years of kisses stored up inside. The few we'd managed to have only served to stoke my need. She was maybe a foot away, so I reined in my body. It wasn't easy being this close to her.

"Hey Amelia," I finally said.

Her throat worked and her cheeks flushed a deeper

shade of pink. Damn. I loved a flustered Amelia. It was a fairly rare occurrence. At least it was before. She was by nature strong and confident. Any chink in that made me feel special. Not because I wanted to fluster her, but because I felt so fucking raw when it came to her, I didn't want to feel alone in it. Knowing maybe she felt vulnerable too eased the uncertainty.

When Amelia didn't respond, Lucy emitted a loud sigh. "Okay, how about I leave you two be?"

Amelia's eyes widened and she tore her gaze from me, a slightly panicked look in her eyes. "Oh no, you don't need to do that. I mean, we have to get back to work and…"

Lucy shook her head. "You're my friend, and I adore you, but you've dug in so deep to avoid this man here…" She pointed at me with a warm smile. "…that it's time to stop that madness. I'll see you in the morning. Let's meet at the office and head out to the Jacobson site together."

I promptly decided Lucy was absolutely awesome. Lucy didn't give Amelia much chance to respond when she quickly stood and grabbed her plate. She leaned over and pecked Amelia on the cheek. "You've got this." Those wide blue eyes swung to me. "And you'd better be on your absolute best behavior. I heard good things about you, so you'd better prove me right."

Lucy's innocent looks didn't match her attitude. I sensed she'd give me hell if I hurt a hair on Amelia's head. I wondered how much she knew about what went down. Seeing as getting an answer now was out of the question, I met her firm gaze and nodded. "Understood."

She grinned. "Have fun kids." She spun away, calling out to Janet, "I need a takeout box, Janet!"

I took a gulp of my coffee and glanced to Amelia. She was worrying her bottom lip, which she needed to stop. Or else I might have more trouble than I already did and end up kissing her right here in front of everyone. No matter how much I knew it seemed like it was for the best Amelia had walked out on her wedding with Earl, I was sensitive to the fact it wouldn't exactly look good for us to make out in the middle of town less than a week later.

She met my gaze. "Hey," she finally said. "Um, how are you?"

I wondered how to respond. Because the answer was complicated. On the one hand, I was great. The one and only woman I'd ever loved wasn't marrying someone else. I'd finally been able to feel her come apart in my arms. While that had done nothing other than ratchet up the lust nearly burning me up inside, it felt so damn good. On the other hand, I was sitting here looking at her and wishing like hell I could bridge the chasm between us. Seven years of bitterness and regret on both sides. To truly get to what I wanted with Amelia, I knew we had to cross that chasm together, or what we had would never hold. Just like it hadn't before.

I stared into her amber eyes, flickering with so much feeling, and tried to collect myself. "I'm okay. You?"

She lifted one shoulder in a shrug. "So-so. It's, uh... Well, it's weird knowing you're here. You're actually here. To stay."

My heart gave a hard kick. I had to keep my emotions in check, so I took another gulp of coffee before replying. "It's weird for me too. It's not what I thought I'd be dealing with though, so that's good."

"What do you mean?"

I laughed, an edge of bitterness in it. "Well, I thought I'd be coming home and getting used to you being married to someone else." I had to pause and clear my throat. "Look, you have to know I didn't know how to do this. I convinced myself I was over you. I missed being here for all kinds of reasons that have nothing to do with you and all kinds of reasons that have everything to do with you. Now I'm here, and it's not what I thought. You're not married, and there's no way in hell I can say I'm over you. But I'd be lying if I said I didn't regret the way things played out and I'm pissed you never gave me a chance to explain."

Her breath drew in sharply, and her eyes glittered with the sheen of tears. Fuck. I was barreling right into the thick of it. Without thinking, I slipped my hand over hers. "Hey, I didn't mean..."

She shook her head sharply. "It's okay. You're just telling it like it is. It's not like we don't both know it."

Her hand was cold under mine, a subtle tremor running through her. I stayed quiet.

After a few beats, she glanced my way again. "Maybe we should just have lunch," she said with a half smile.

I couldn't keep from grinning. Emotions might be running in fits and starts inside, but the overriding truth was I was home and Amelia was here with me.

Chapter Thirteen
AMELIA

I leaned my hips against the counter and crossed my arms, fighting the urge to swear.

My mother, Sarah Haynes, stood at the kitchen sink attacking the dishes. My mom was a usually calm person, but one thing that annoyed her to no end: drama. At present, she was taking her frustration out on me hightailing out of my wedding on the dishes.

"I still can't believe it," my mom said, her dark hair streaked with gray swinging to and fro. She rinsed another plate and set it forcefully into the dish rack before turning around. She snagged a towel to dry her hands, pinning me with her dark brown gaze. "I wish you'd saved yourself the trouble and not gone so far into the whole wedding thing."

"Mom, I know it's a mess. I'm sorry. I really am. But the only person I need to apologize to is Earl and he's already gone fishing," I replied, beating back the annoyance with myself for letting things go so far in the first place.

My mom's gaze coasted over me. After a moment, her eyes softened on a sigh. "I'm sorry hon. You're absolutely right. The only person you owe any apology to is Earl, and

I'm not even so sure about that. Honestly, the way he handled the whole thing—it was like no big deal. I had my doubts about you two before, but after that..." Her eyes flashed with anger. "I'm not upset you called the wedding off. I'm upset you put yourself through it all."

My mom stepped away from the counter, snagging her walking cane leaning against it as she did. She'd been in a bad car accident two years ago, resulting in a broken hip, a shattered femur and a broken ankle. She'd healed up well, but she'd never quite gotten her walking back to where it had been. She hated it to no end because she'd always lived an active life, but she'd adjusted.

I followed her over to the kitchen table and sat down across from her, resting my chin in my hand. "I get it, Mom. I wish I'd figured it all out a lot sooner. Lucy told me Earl didn't even seem that upset."

My mom nodded slowly as she sipped on a cup of coffee she'd left here a few minutes prior. "Not so much. Oh, I think it stung him a little, but that's about it. How are you though?"

I considered the question and shrugged. The answer was too confusing. At moments, I was overwhelmed with relief at ending things with Earl. In others, I was awash in elation at knowing Cade was back and realizing maybe we could repair the mess we'd made of things. I swung between poles of elation and terror. I didn't think I could handle trying with Cade again and having it fall apart. I'd never recovered before. Hell, I'd blocked out the pain so completely, I couldn't even tolerate talking about him and somehow managed to avoid learning the truth of what happened with Shannon. Nothing. The betrayal was Shannon's alone.

I couldn't seem to banish the niggling doubts from her manipulation. See, the thing was Shannon was the kind of girl most guys chased after. She was pretty, definitely not Amazon-like as I was, and feminine. Honestly, if we hadn't been friends from when we were kids, it's not likely we'd have ended up friends. By the time high school rolled around, she was all kinds of girly, while I was still pretty tomboy and just didn't have it in me to play those games.

My mother's perceptive gaze coasted over me. "Cade drove you back to Willow Brook," she said, a statement of fact rather than a question.

At my nod, she asked, "Don't suppose you'd like to talk about that?"

I shrugged and marshaled my wits. "It's kinda hard to talk about when him showing up is like being struck by a bolt of lightning."

My mom smiled softly. "I bet it is. I'm taking it as a good thing you didn't change the subject when I said his name."

I managed a laugh, but it hurt. I'd been so damn determined to change the subject when it came to Cade, I'd missed a few important details.

My mom angled her head to the side. "Well, I kept my distance before because you didn't let me do anything else. Now he's back and here to stay from what I hear from Georgia, I'll say my piece. You loved that man like crazy and never got over him. Don't be so stupid and stubborn again."

I stared at her, fighting the urge to argue. After a moment, I nodded. "Let's just say I'm trying not to. Good enough?"

I only hoped I could manage to get through to the other side of my doubts.

My mom arched a brow. "It's your life, but I love you and it was awful to see you so torn up. Cade was gone, so it didn't seem worth dredging up the mess before."

I was relieved when my mother's phone started chirping from where it sat in the middle of the table. She flashed a grin. "Saved by your brother," she said as she glanced down at the screen and picked up the phone.

"Hey Quinn," she said.

She nodded along at something Quinn said, her eyes flicking to me. "Your sister's sitting right here. Like I told you, she came back home two days later after a hideaway night at your place."

"Tell him I said hey," I offered.

She held a finger up as she listened to Quinn. "She says to tell you hey."

At that, my mom handed the phone over. I didn't have much choice, so I took the phone, lifting it to my ear. "How's it going, Quinn?"

"Well I'm fine, but how are you?" he countered.

I could imagine his concerned gaze. I'd always felt lucky when it came to my brother. He was a good guy all around.

"I'm fine," I replied, not sure what else to offer after my rather dramatic weekend. I was supposed to be on my honeymoon now, but was nowhere near that. In the span of a few minutes, I'd turned my planned life on its head. I was so relieved, just thinking about it sent another wave of relief through me.

Quinn chuckled softly. "That's what Mom said. Good to know. Next time you decide to bolt on your wedding day, how about not giving Mom a heart attack and calling one of us back?"

I bit back a sigh, a wash of guilt rolling through me.

"Quinn, I'm sorry. I really am. I wasn't thinking too clearly and chucked my phone. It was Earl I didn't want to deal with, but I didn't think about much else."

"I figured as much. Anyway, guess I can say now it seems like it's best?"

I leaned back in my chair and traced the grain of the wood on the table. "It is. It was right before I needed to go in, and I just couldn't."

"Okay then. I just want you to be okay, so as long as you're okay, I'm good. Lacey said to tell you to call if you need to talk."

I smiled, emotion clogging my throat. Even if it might chafe, I knew I was blessed to have family that cared. "Tell her I just might. Right now, I'm laying low and trying to get back to my life."

"Good enough then. If you need to stay at the cabin more than one night, it's all yours."

"Thanks Quinn. I chopped plenty of wood for you."

Amidst his laugh, he said goodbye. I stayed a bit longer to help my mother take care of a few things in the yard and then headed to the office. Cade had taken up residence in my thoughts, so whenever I wasn't busy, he was filling my mind. He had a commanding presence, and I felt caught in the tides of a powerful pull toward him. When I wasn't busy worrying over how to get through to the other side of seven long years marred by a misunderstanding and our shared stubbornness, I was fantasizing about him. Just now, heat rolled through me, recalling the feel of his lips on mine and his fingers buried inside of me.

Chapter Fourteen
CADE

I walked into the Willow Brook Fire Station and up to the reception desk where a young woman was on the phone. I'd never seen her before. Before I'd left for my hot shot training, I'd volunteered here regularly. Carol Rogers had been the nerve center of the dispatch here back then and for as long as I could remember. She'd passed away about a year ago, and I'd been sad to find out I was too late to make it to her funeral. I'd been out in the field dealing with a dangerous fire in the Sierra Mountains at the time. Carol had been like a grandmother to me, along with many of the firefighters who passed through here.

The young woman who appeared to be her replacement had curly brown hair barely tamed into a ponytail and wide brown eyes. She finished her call and looked at me over the counter. "Hi, can I help you?" she asked, her tone cool. She certainly lacked Carol's warm, motherly manner.

"Cade Masters. I'm here to drop off my gear before I start next week."

Her expression didn't change, but she nodded. "Okay. Let me see if anyone's expecting you."

Slightly annoyed, I shrugged. So much for a warm welcome.

She picked up the phone and paged the back. I heard her mention my name and then nod. After she hung up, she stood and walked around the desk to open the door leading to the back. "Come on back," she said, waving her hand into the hallway.

I stepped through and felt a sense of homecoming wash over me. I'd been home for a few days, but coming here was a second layer of it for me. I'd spent most of my adolescence bouncing around this place. With my father as the police chief and the police offices one building over, I was almost always running around nearby. Once I'd gotten my hot shot training out of the way, I'd always had half an eye on the jobs here.

I might've wanted to avoid the pain of seeing Amelia settle down with someone else, but I'd missed Willow Brook and my dream had been to be part of the hot shot crew here. Willow Brook had a local firefighting crew, which wasn't too big because the town wasn't large. However, the fire station here served as a base for two hotshot crews, so it was busy here. They had federal and state teams flying in and out of Willow Brook during the height of fire season. In recent years, fires out West, Alaska included, had increased markedly, so hotshot teams were in demand. We were the only teams specially trained to function independently in isolated wilderness and rough terrain. I'd taken a foreman position for one of the crews and was ready to start. I was slated to officially be on duty next week, but I had gear to drop off and wanted to see who was around.

The young woman barely cracked a smile as she waited for me to pass and turned to close the door behind us. I couldn't help but notice she was a bundle of curves. I might not feel a thing, what with Amelia permanently lodged in my brain these days, but I could appreciate this woman was a likely distraction here at the station. Well, except for the fact she was cranky as hell. I decided to push her a little.

"So I'm Cade. Don't think I've seen you around before." I held my hand out.

"I'm Maisie Rogers," she said, her voice flat as she shook my hand.

"You wouldn't be any relation to Carol Rogers?" I asked as I dropped her hand and started to follow her down the hall.

"She was my grandma," Maisie replied, the slightest softening to her tone.

"Really? You must not have grown up here, or I'd know you."

A curl bounced as she shook her head. "Nope. My mom went to college in San Francisco and never moved back. Grandma left me her house when she passed away. I didn't plan on ending up in her job, but they hadn't filled it yet when I got here. I figured I could fill in and now I'm still here."

We reached the door into the back and Maisie pushed through, stopping abruptly by the door.

The back area was as I remembered it—lockers, gear hanging in tidy rows, and a kitchen and hang out area to the back.

"Cade!" a voice called out.

The man in question turned from where he was by the kitchen counter and strode my way.

"Beck, man. Good to see you! I wasn't sure you were still here," I replied as we met halfway across the room.

Beck pulled me into a quick hug and stepped back, flashing a lazy grin. "Course I'm here. I'm foreman for the other crew. How ya been?"

Beck Steele had gone to high school with me. We'd run in the same circles, although Beck hadn't started as a firefighter before I left town. I heard he was here through the grapevine. Beck was a good guy. Solid, steady and always good for a laugh. He didn't take himself, or anyone else, too seriously. With his black curls and green eyes, the girls had chased after him in high school. As far as I knew, he'd never been caught by any of them. He enjoyed the chase and that was about it.

"Doin' alright. It's good to be home," I replied.

"Good to have you here. You met Maisie, right?" Beck asked in return, glancing between us.

Maisie nodded, her curly ponytail bouncing. The incongruity of that with her cool expression made me want to laugh.

"Yup, we met," I offered.

Beck shrugged, another lazy grin. "Of course." He glanced to me. "We miss Carol like crazy, but Maisie's almost as bossy as her."

Maisie's eyes narrowed, and her cheeks turned pink. She opened her mouth to say something when the radio hooked to her belt beeped. She snagged it and hurried back through the door to the front.

I glanced from the door back to Beck. "She might be bossy like Carol, but.... Not exactly warm and fuzzy."

Beck shrugged and rolled his eyes. "Yeah, we're still trying to warm her up."

I scanned the room, circling back to Beck. "So, I brought some gear to drop off. Okay if I go ahead and bring it in?"

"Of course, let me give a hand."

In short order, I had hung my gear in a locker, met a few of the other guys and caught up with Beck. Beck walked me back out to his truck and leaned against the tailgate. "So, what finally brought you back?" he asked.

"Been meaning to come back for a while. When I saw the foreman position open up, I jumped at it."

I left unsaid that I'd stayed away as long as I had, in part because I'd been deep into avoiding Amelia and everything that fell apart between us.

Beck eyed me and nodded slowly. "Guessing you heard your girl up and left Earl Osborne at the altar."

I ran a hand through my hair. "Amelia hasn't been my girl for a long time."

Beck chuckled. "Whatever, man. I love this place, but word travels. Already heard you're the one who brought her back to town after she bolted at her wedding. Just a heads up, if I heard about it, well, that means the whole damn town did."

I kicked my heel against a tire. I'd missed many things about Willow Brook, but gossip wasn't one of them. "Aw hell. Don't tell me I'm gonna have to face people pissed off at me. All I did was run into her at a bar. Damn woman managed to start a fistfight," I said with a chuckle.

Beck threw his head back with a laugh. "That must've been a sight."

"Oh yeah. I walk in and see her land her fist right in some guy's face. Next thing I know, he knocks her right to the ground." I paused and shook my head. "So, I waded in there and got her out of the way. Had no idea she'd just walked out on Earl, although the fact she was wearing a wedding dress tipped me off."

Beck shook his head. "Well, she's given the gossips something to chew on for a few months between walking out on Earl and you coming back to town."

"Oh hell. I hate that shit," I replied.

Beck eyed me for a beat. "Right, well at least it's Earl. He's so laid back about everything, I doubt he'll much care. Far as I'm concerned, just goes to show she was right to walk out."

Beck's cell phone beeped, and he glanced at the screen. "Gotta take this. Trying to buy some land and it's the bank. How about you meet up with me and the guys this Saturday at Wildlands?"

"Will do," I replied as Beck gave a nod and took the call.

I turned and looked across the street once Beck disappeared inside. Willow Brook was one of the older towns in Alaska, established during the mythical gold rush era. The original fire station had been renovated into the Firehouse Café, while this newer building was built back when I was a boy. It was square and utilitarian, but situated right on Main Street with a nice view of Swan Lake.

The sun glinted off the lake with its namesake Trumpeter swans drifting in the center. The swans came every summer, decorating the lake as they floated regally in its waters. I looked out over the water and took a breath. I'd missed this view, missed so many things. I was partially kicking myself for holding out this long before coming home. Yet, in the back of my mind, I knew I'd have felt a hell of a lot differently if I were here dealing with the reality of Amelia with someone else like a punch to my gut. I might be gnawing on a lot of emotions over her, but the barren pain of thinking she was out of reach was gone.

I glanced at my watch. I figured it was time to track her down.

Chapter Fifteen
AMELIA

"What do you mean you can't get out here until next week?" I asked into my phone.

"Amelia, I'm sorry. My excavator took some damage last week when a tractor-trailer clipped it on the way back from Anchorage. Trust me when I say I'm as annoyed as you about the whole mess," Max replied.

Max Richards was the guy I usually subcontracted with for excavation work. It wasn't a full-time gig for him. In fact, it was very part-time. He was a biologist for the federal government, but like most everyone in Alaska, he had several irons in the fire. After getting burned by a few of the more full-time crews around here who thought I was stupid enough to trust their rates, I'd heard Max did this work on the side and called him up. He was an old friend of Quinn's, and I trusted him completely. He charged fair rates and his pace worked with mine. With my small two-woman crew, I stayed busy, but I didn't line up too many projects.

I paced back and forth in front of my work truck, considering what to do. "When will it be ready?"

"Next week. If you can wait, I'll be at the site Monday," Max replied.

Knowing I couldn't get anyone else in on such short notice without paying a fortune for an emergency job, I figured it was best to wait. "That'll have to work."

"Thanks Amelia. See you then," Max said before ending the call.

I tucked my phone in my pocket and glanced around for Lucy. I caught sight of Lucy's blonde hair peeking out from under her baseball cap over by the stream running through the corner of the lot. I strode over to find her leaning over with her face practically in the stream.

"Okay Lucy, *what* are you doing?"

Lucy glanced up quickly before looking back into the stream. "Look! There's some small trout in here," Lucy said, pointing to the stream where all I could see was the sun glinting off its surface.

I stepped closer and leaned down to see trout hovering in the water in a small eddy created by the rocks. "Nice. Wonder if the Jacobson's are into fishing?"

Lucy straightened and shrugged. "Maybe. Have you met them yet?"

The Jacobson's were the couple that had hired me to build their house after a recommendation from none other than Cade's father. I shook my head. "Nope. They've visited here in the summer, but haven't come up yet this year. They plan to be here next month, so here's hoping they don't mind a week's delay on the project."

Lucy's eyes narrowed. "What do you mean?"

"Max's excavator got a little dinged up when a tractor-trailer hit clipped him on the highway. He says he can be here next week, but until then..." I shrugged. "Not much for us to do. All the plans are ready, but we can't build until the land is ready, so we wait. Let's split up for today. How about you take care of finishing up the decking on the job on the far side of town? I'll go meet with that couple that wants to draw up plans for a house. I think it's a little late to start this year, but they want to get the process going. Sound like a plan?"

We turned and started walking back toward my work truck together. Lucy idly kicked a pebble as we walked. "Works for me. Do you think it's worth seeing if someone else can handle the excavation on short notice?"

"Not unless I want to pay through the nose. Plus, Max does good work and never tries to cut corners. I'd rather deal with a delay than worry about someone squeezing the job in and not getting it right."

We stopped when we reached the truck. Lucy started to say something and stopped when we heard the sound of tires coming down the gravel drive leading through the trees. "Who would be...?" Lucy started to ask before a grin spread across her face.

My back had been to the drive, so I glanced over my shoulder to see Cade's truck rolling up to us. My pulse lunged, and my belly did a slow flip.

Cade parked beside my truck and climbed out. My eyes ate him up. I couldn't help it. I was near starved to see him. Seven years of swatting him out of my thoughts had only led to seven years of stored up longing. To have him here, in the flesh, and to recall the feel of his lips on mine while his fingers drove me to near madness—I was instantly hot and bothered.

He wore faded black jeans paired with a black t-shirt, basically a uniform for him, both of which did nothing to hide his hard muscled form. My mouth went dry when his eyes landed on me, his green gaze darkening in a flash. I forgot Lucy was standing right there until Lucy cleared her throat, so audibly it made me flush.

I tore my eyes free from Cade and looked to Lucy, grasping for some semblance of casual. "So, uh..."

Lucy cut in, looking between us. "Cade, you mind giving Amelia a ride to her office?"

Confused, I stared at her. "What? No, I've got work to do. I'll..."

"I'm the one who needs the truck. I'll pick up the decking and head out to finish up that job. You don't need the truck. This way, I don't have to go through town," Lucy said matter-of-factly.

Lucy had a perfectly reasonable point, yet I didn't miss the subtle teasing gleam in her eyes. Before I had a chance to reply, Cade beat me to it.

"Sounds like you're riding with me then. Wouldn't want Lucy to waste time on a trip to town," he said.

His gruff voice sent a shiver through me. *This is ridiculous. All he's doing is talking and you're practically panting.* I shushed my internal critic and glanced between Lucy and Cade. I was torn between two urges—the urge to flee because Cade brought up all kinds of feelings inside and I wasn't so sure I knew how to handle them, and the urge to fling myself at him and forget the rest of the world.

When I didn't say anything, Lucy reached over and snagged the keys right out of my hand. "That's settled then. Text me about our schedule tomorrow."

Lucy, being Lucy, moved fast and hopped in the truck inside of a few seconds, leaving me to wave as she backed up and turned the truck around. I watched the Kick A** Construction tailgate fade from sight as Lucy drove swiftly down the driveway.

My heart set to pounding hard and fast. Being alone with Cade was something I craved so, it sent my body into overdrive and my emotions spinning wildly. On the heels of a deep breath and a complete failure to slow my pulse, I looked over at Cade. He was looking around, giving me a moment to look at him. His brown curls were mussed, as they almost always were. I followed the strong line of his jaw and down his neck and along his muscled chest, my eyes drawn to the edge of his collar where his tanned skin tempted me to lean over and lick it.

Really? You can't be thinking like this. You were nearly ruined by this man. Even if it wasn't what you thought it was, don't fall right back to a place where you can't keep it together.

Another swat at my thoughts. I didn't need to wrestle with myself when I had Cade standing here.

"Nice site to build," Cade commented as his gaze made its way back to me. "Whose property?"

I scanned the area. It was a lovely lot with the building site nestled in a forested area with a mix of blue spruce, cottonwood and birch. The stream where Lucy noticed the trout ran along one side of the property with the trees thinning to the other side and offering a distant view of Swan Lake. I looked up at Cade and nodded. "It's a great place. A couple from out of state snapped this land up when the timber company sold some lots off a few years ago. Your dad actually gave the Jacobson's my name last year."

Cade nodded slowly, holding my gaze and sending my belly into a dizzying series of flips. He'd never shied away from eye contact. He used to drive me wild with nothing but a look back in the heady days of our youthful love. He hadn't lost his touch. Whether it was him or my own ridiculous weakness for him, I didn't know. He was quiet, everything around us fading. I distantly heard the rustle of squirrels in the trees and an irate magpie chattering, but my entire body spun toward Cade. It was as if he was a magnetic force for me.

My breath became shallow and I tried to rein my body in, but it was an exercise in futility. Heat coiled in my belly and radiated outward. Cade angled to face me and reached up to remove my baseball cap. I'd tucked my hair up underneath it, and it tumbled free. He lifted a hand and slid his fingers through the ends of it. He didn't say a word. The air around us hummed to life, while desire rolled through me in a wave. Hot shivers chased over my skin.

He stepped closer, winding my hair around his hand, reeling me closer with every breath I could barely take.

"Cade, what are you doing?" My voice was raspy and breathy.

"This," he said, the word fierce and definitive, before his lips crashed against mine.

The point of contact was like a bolt of fire. It galvanized me. My desire and tumult of emotions were nearly burning me up inside—the only relief was to dive into the flames with him.

Our tongues dueled—our kiss rough, hot and wet. He brought me flush against him, his cock hot and hard against me, while his hands roved roughly over me. I couldn't get close enough, my hands greedily exploring him, sliding up under his shirt and savoring every hard muscled plane and the warmth of his skin.

I wasn't conscious of anything I was doing until he gentled our kiss, slowly drawing back. His lips dusted along my jaw and down my neck. My skin pebbled in response, and I fought to catch my breath when he paused, his lips against my skin in the curve where my neck met my shoulder. I became conscious enough to realize I had one hand curled over his cock through his jeans and the other gripping his back, holding him tight against me. My body didn't want any space between us, not even an increment. Neither did my heart.

My mind? Well, therein lay the problem. Every time I thought, I felt as if I was wading through seven years of the mangled emotions that followed what I'd believed had been his betrayal. Thrown into the mix now was my own guilt at having shut him out so completely and cutting myself off from even trying to find out what happened.

"I think maybe I should give you that ride," Cade murmured into my neck.

I felt his lips move against my skin when he spoke, and it sent heat streaking through me. I held still because I couldn't bring myself to move away just yet.

His heart pounded in time with mine, and I took a small

bit of relief in knowing at least I wasn't alone in my response. After a few beats, he slowly drew back, straightening, his eyes colliding with mine. He lifted a hand and brushed my hair away from my forehead. "So?"

Through the haze of desire, I stared at him, trying to compute.

"Should we go?" he asked, puncturing the haze just enough I could think.

"Probably," I finally said.

His mouth hooked at one corner. Damn, I'd forgotten how devastating his half-smiles could be. I'd barely gotten my body under control, and now another wave of need rolled through me.

When he didn't move away, I finally moved my hand off of his cock. I didn't want to, I really didn't, but this was beyond ridiculous. I should be able to act like I had some kind of control. Even though my memories of what things had been like before with us were nothing but good except for the end, I didn't recall feeling this wildly out of control.

He finally stepped back, his hand sliding down my arm and curling around one of mine. "Let's go."

Moments later, I was watching the landscape roll by as Cade drove back toward downtown Willow Brook. A flock of sandhill cranes was scattered about a field, their distinct red crowns standing out amidst the tall grasses. The ride to town was quiet. I was about to tell Cade where my office was when he turned into the parking lot behind it.

When I'd first started my business, I hadn't ever thought I'd need an office. I kept picking up jobs here and there and took care of the business end of things at home. My business expanded from small jobs to jobs where I actually needed to put my architecture skills to work, and it didn't work too well to have clients showing up at my home. I rented a small office around the corner from the fire station. The building housed an office supply business on the lower floor and a few offices upstairs.

Cade turned his truck off, and quiet settled around us. My pulse had barely started to calm on the short drive here. In the weighted quiet, it skittered wildly. When I looked toward him, he was looking out the window, his gaze inscrutable. As if he sensed me looking his way, he turned to face me. I swallowed and tried to quell the butterflies spinning in my belly.

"I suppose you have work to do," he finally said.

"A little. Um, when are you starting work?"

"Next week."

I felt myself nodding, while I wondered what to say next. I hated this tension between us. There was the good tension linked to the off the charts, seven years of pent up longing, and then the threads of tension tightening after too many years of unresolved messiness between us.

He knocked me off the loop in my brain when he spoke. "Don't suppose you have a bathroom?"

A laugh bubbled up. "Come on." I waved for him to follow as I climbed out and made my way inside. Up a flight of stairs from the back hallway, I led him into my office.

"Bathroom's right through there," I said, gesturing to the door in the hallway.

I walked into my office and glanced around the room. It was a single room with a drafting table, a desk and a small table with chairs for reviewing plans with clients. I surprised myself by spending a decent amount of time here. I usually met Lucy here several mornings each week and often spent a few hours in the evenings when I needed to catch up on the business end of things. I strolled over to the windows and looked outside. The sun was high in the sky and the street below suddenly busy with traffic backed up behind a slow moving camper. Alaska roads became crowded every summer with massive campers cluttering them.

My phone vibrated in my pocket, and I answered it without even looking at the screen.

"Hey Amelia." Earl's low voice rumbled through the line.

My stomach knotted with tension. I'd already apologized when I dumped him right before our not-wedding, but I'd been dreading the next time I spoke to him. I cursed myself for not bothering to check to see who was calling. It would have been nice to be mentally prepared, not to mention Cade would be walking in any second now.

"Hi Earl. How's your fishing trip?" I asked, unable to keep the bite out of my tone.

I might be completely relieved to have ended things once and for all, and I hadn't wanted to hurt him, yet it was too reinforcing to have him so easily swing back into his life as if nothing was amiss. While it backed up every second doubt I'd had for most of the time we'd dated, it didn't mean it felt good knowing that's how little of an effect I had on him.

"Fishing's great. Thought I'd check in and see how you were doing," he returned.

If he was the least bit ruffled over what had happened, I couldn't tell.

"I'm fine. I stopped by to talk when I got back to town, but everyone who might know told me you'd taken off on a fishing trip with Dan."

"Yep. We went up toward the Yukon River. We're heading back the day after tomorrow, so I thought maybe we could grab dinner tomorrow at Wildlands."

I was taken aback, but I immediately realized I should've expected something like this from Earl. I figured I owed him dinner at the least.

I heard the bathroom door open and close from the hallway and Cade's footsteps coming into my office. I studiously kept my attention out the windows. I had nothing to hide, so I wasn't going to act like I did.

"Sure. Where?"

"Let's meet at Wildlands. Say 7?"

"Okay."

I sensed him expecting me to say more, but Cade or not, I didn't have much else to say. I didn't particularly want to have dinner with him, but I figured the least I could do was offer more of an explanation than my hurried one before I dashed into the rain.

After a moment of quiet, during which I could feel Cade walking across the room to me, Earl said, "Okay, see you then."

"Okay. Have a safe trip back."

I ended the call quickly, swiping the screen off and glancing to Cade.

His features were tight, and I knew in a flash he was angry.

He was dead silent for a moment as he stared out the windows and then flicked his eyes to me. "That was Earl," he said, a statement rather than a question.

Chapter Sixteen

CADE

A flash of anger and jealousy roared through me as I stood there looking at Amelia. What the hell was she doing on the phone with Earl?

If I'd been feeling sensible, I'd have considered that last I knew, she'd bolted from her wedding and not even given Earl much of an explanation. But I wasn't feeling sensible. I was feeling plain territorial. It didn't matter we hadn't bridged the chasm of years of regret and longing between us. It didn't matter that I'd had absolutely no plans to get involved with anyone seriously ever again—because Amelia had been off limits in my brain ever since I'd heard she was engaged. It didn't matter that I didn't really know what she wanted—as far as the concept of 'want' functioned in a calm, rational manner.

Nothing mattered except what I knew in my heart and soul. Amelia was mine and always had been. No other man had any claim to her.

Her eyes searched my face, a subtly mutinous look entering her gaze. I knew that look. She was stubborn and whatever she thought I might be thinking, she was getting ready to argue about it.

Hot anger, jealousy and pure lust driving me, I caught her hand in mine and yanked her to me. Sliding one hand over her lush bottom, I pressed her against my arousal and slammed my mouth against hers. She gasped, and I dove into her mouth. Our kiss exploded into a wet tangle of lips, teeth and tongues. Holding her tight against me, I threaded my other hand into her hair as I devoured her mouth.

She didn't hold back, and I loved that about her. Her tongue warred with mine as she flexed into me. Fire roared through me, our kiss getting rougher and wilder with every second. The sound of footsteps in the hallway through the open doorway barely filtered into my consciousness.

"Hey Amelia, are you…"

Whoever was walking into Amelia's office came to an abrupt stop, just as Amelia tore her mouth away from mine. We broke apart as abruptly as we'd come together. I stared at her, unable to tear my eyes away. Her breath was heaving, right along with mine, and her cheeks were flushed. Her lips were swollen from our bruising kiss, and I didn't give a damn we'd just given someone a show.

"Wow, sorry for the interruption, but you two just made my day."

Amelia snapped her head toward the door, just as I did. Janet from the Firehouse Café stood there with a sly grin on her face. Amelia's cheeks flushed a deeper shade of pink, making me want to yank her right back against me. I shackled my urges and tried to slow the banging of my heart.

"Janet, what's up?" Amelia managed to ask, her voice husky.

Janet glanced between us, her grin never wavering. "Nothing at all." With a wink, she spun around and closed the door behind her.

I looked back to Amelia. For several beats, we simply stood there. She was so close, I could easily reach over and pull her right back to me. I didn't. I wanted her so fiercely, yet I needed to get control. I was letting burning lust and raw need drive everything. My control was frayed and the jealousy that sent me crashing into her was still simmering. I forced myself to take a slow breath.

After a moment, I thought I could manage myself. "I, uh…"

Just what did I mean to say? Hell if I knew.

Muddled and irritated with myself for being so at the mercy of her, I stepped back and slipped my hands in my pockets. "I'm guessing you need to get to work. I've got a few things to take care of, so I'll go."

I started to turn when her voice stopped me.

"Cade."

I glanced back, arching a brow.

"I didn't call Earl. He called me," she said simply.

I nodded and kept my damn mouth shut. I was acting like a fucking fool over her, and I didn't like it. Not one bit.

"It doesn't mean anything," she added.

I realized she was expecting me to say something.

"I don't have any right to get pissed about Earl, so you don't need to explain." I paused, my thoughts spinning back to the day Amelia had walked in at the worst possible moment. It didn't matter that it had all been Shannon's doing. I had a glimmer of what she must've felt like back then. I was chewed up inside over nothing other than a phone call from the man I knew she'd left.

She was still watching me, and I wanted to step to her and wrap her in my arms and forget the knotted mess of emotions we'd never had a chance to untangle. Now we had that chance, but it was going to take some doing.

"Now I know how you felt that day you saw Shannon trying to climb in bed with me."

Her eyes widened and her breath drew in sharply. A heaviness filled the space between us, and my heart ached, literally.

"Maybe so," she said softly.

Footsteps sounded in the hallway again. I marshaled my sanity and stepped to her again. Dipping my head, I dropped a quick kiss on her lips, forcing myself to draw back immediately. "I'm supposed to meet the guys Saturday at Wildlands. How about you meet me there later?"

I figured perhaps we should try to do something normal and maybe that would help. Amelia's eyes flashed with something and then she shook her head slowly. "I just told Earl I'd meet him for dinner. It's not a date. I just figured I owed him an explanation for bolting from our wedding."

Her words might as well have been static for all I could hear with the hot jealousy that shot through me. I couldn't do this, couldn't fucking do it. I spun away and stalked out of her office.

Chapter Seventeen
AMELIA

I started to run after him, but came to an abrupt stop when I saw Cade's mother in the doorway. Her footsteps must have been the ones we heard approaching. Georgia Masters flicked her eyes from Cade to me. Whatever might be passing through her mind, she kept to herself as she glanced up to Cade. Cade kept walking, his head down.

I fought the tears pressing hot against the back of my eyes. Georgia looked toward me as Cade's boots sounded on the stairs. I held myself back from dashing past Georgia and took in a gulp of air.

The door slammed shut, its sound echoing all the way up the stairs. Georgia's assessing gaze scanned me. Long before Cade and I had gotten involved, Georgia had been close to a second mother to me. Being good friends with my own mother meant Georgia was around often and babysat for my brother and me when we were little. After Cade had moved away and things had ended on such an ugly note, it had been hard to be around Georgia.

After a few overtures at first, Georgia stopped trying to talk to me about Cade and let me stew in my own anger. I wished for about the thousandth time in the last week or so that I hadn't been so damn stubborn for so long. My firm refusal to talk about anything to do with Cade meant I'd never found out the truth of Shannon's full ownership of that betrayal.

Georgia angled her head toward my office and walked toward the table. I followed her, if anything because I didn't know what else to do. Georgia sat down at the small circular table. "Sit down dear," she said firmly.

I sat down across from her, resting my elbows on the table and tunneling my hands through my hair.

"Okay, are we allowed to talk about Cade now?" Georgia asked pointedly.

I met her sharp green gaze and nodded.

Georgia was quiet for a beat. "You love him and he loves you. You both messed up because you're both stubborn as hell."

I swallowed against the emotion knotting in my chest and throat. "Did you always know he'd never had anything to do with Shannon?"

Georgia nodded slowly. "At first, it was only because I knew my son would never do anything like that. Later, the rumors died down and I sorted out what happened. I didn't try to talk to you about it back then. By then, he was far away in California, and honey, you weren't having it. So I let it go. He moved on and it seemed like you did too. Trust me, I wanted to meddle, but it didn't seem fair to either one of you."

I let my hands slide out of my hair and traced a fingertip along the curved edge of the table. I wished like hell she'd been unfair and meddled, but it was way too late to do anything about that.

"I can't figure out how to fix it now. I was mad for so long and it was all over the wrong thing. I'm still pissed at Shannon, but now I'm just as pissed off at myself." I paused to catch my breath. Emotion was barreling through me so hard and fast, I felt lightheaded. "He, uh... He got upset because I told him I'd agreed to have dinner with Earl. It's not a date. I just figure I owe Earl more of an explanation than the one I gave him before I left him behind at our wedding."

Georgia drummed her fingers on the table and sighed. "Of course you do. I might think you finally made the right decision for yourself and, frankly, for Earl too. But if he wants a few minutes of your time, he should get it. Earl might not have ever appreciated you for who you were—at least, that's how I saw it—but he's not a bad guy. He's just..." She pursed her lips as if considering how to describe what she meant. "He's a guy's guy and he's pretty simple. I don't mean he's stupid, just basic in how he thinks. You are, well, let me put it this way. You intimate most men because you're so strong, so independent and so beautiful. He wanted to show he wasn't cowed by any of that, but he didn't see past that. Cade will simmer down. He lied to himself about being over you. That much I know. Take it as a good thing he's so pissed off. That man loves you to pieces. He's never been one to do anything in half-measures. Give him a little time."

I managed to nod, but my heart felt like it was splintering. I moved to tracing a file folder sitting on the table, my eyes following the lines. After a moment, I managed to look up and almost burst into tears. I hated feeling vulnerable, I hated it so much I'd walled Cade and anything to do with him out of my life. Now it was coming back to bite me, and the caring look on Georgia's face only reminded me how much it hurt.

Georgia reached across the table, catching my hand and giving it a squeeze. "It's okay to feel like this. When we love someone, sometimes it's hard. You and Cade had it pretty easy back then. Nothing ruffled the surface, so it seemed easy. It's never easy even when it's good. Things come up and you have to get through them. You two are way overdue on this one and both of you have some feelings bottled up. Just give it time. Okay?"

I took a slow breath, the warmth in Georgia's words filtering through the reflexive anxiety I felt. By no means did I feel great about where things were at, but maybe, just maybe, Cade and I would get through this.

The following evening, I stared across the table at Earl. I'd managed to be polite, but he was pissing me off. At this point, I was wondering how I'd ever even thought he was anything other than an arrogant jerk. I practically had skid marks on my tongue from keeping my mouth shut. The only thing keeping me at the table now was the fact I figured his pride had taken a hit and that was why he was being an ass. I'd give him this dinner and that would be it.

That said, I was annoyed enough, I couldn't help but needle him.

"So, fishing trip, huh?" I asked.

I didn't want Earl, but him so easily bouncing back after I left him behind, well, it was sand in an old wound. A wound that had nothing to do with him, yet everything about our failed relationship was like a neon sign pointing to those old feelings of insecurity. Aside from Cade, no man ever made me feel as if I mattered much. To Earl, I mattered so little, I could dump him minutes before our wedding and he shifted gears so fast it was like a spotlight on how little I meant.

Earl looked across the table at me and shrugged. His mouth hooked at one corner in a grin. As if it was funny somehow.

"Amelia, you left. What the hell was I supposed to do? You've had a bit to cool down, so let's be real. I don't know what happened, but we had a good thing. Let's talk things over and get back to where we were. I think you just freaked because..."

My blood was boiling. A rushing sound muted the voices

around me. I gave my head a shake. Earl reached across the table and grabbed my hand. I shook it off, drawing back.

"Earl, we're not getting back to anything. I meant what I said that day. I never should've said yes."

He stared back at me, his eyes flat and hard to read. Lucy's comments about his pride were becoming more and more obvious.

Chapter Eighteen
CADE

I rolled my truck to a stop in front of Wildlands. Wildlands Lodge was a wilderness guiding and fishing resort on Willow Brook Street, which ran perpendicular to Main Street with Swan Lake a stone's throw away. Willow Brook had been named after a small brook running out of the mountains in the distance. It ran alongside its namesake street before meandering its way to Swan Lake. Wildlands had once been just a bar and restaurant. When the town was feeling left out of the oil boom in the eighties, the owners turned their sights on the slew of people moving to the state and the tourists following them. Wildlands was a destination wilderness lodge now, bringing tourists willing to pay crazy money for fishing and guiding in the area.

It was a modern style wilderness lodge with cedar siding and gorgeous stone chimneys flanking either end of its main building. The hotel portion was in the back with docks adjacent to Swan Lake. I made my way inside, a sense of familiarity washing over me. I'd spent many a night here with friends and with Amelia. The restaurant was packed, crowded with locals and tourists. I scanned the crowd and threaded my way to the bar in the back. The interior had a modern woodsy feel with polished wooden tables scattered throughout and photographs of the Alaskan wilderness and various fishing photos lining the walls.

I caught sight of Beck over in the corner with a few other guys whom I assumed were firefighters. After weaving through the crowd, I slipped into the chair Beck patted beside him.

"Hey man, it's packed here tonight," I offered in greeting.

Beck flashed a grin. "This is the way it is all summer now. Ever since they finished the addition to the lodge here, it's crazy busy."

"When did they do that?" I asked.

"Two summers ago. Added another one hundred rooms. It's nuts. Anyway, let me introduce you. Guys, this is Cade, the new foreman." He gestured to a man with dark blonde hair and bright blue eyes. "Levi Phillips is on your crew." Levi tipped his head in my direction. "Then we have Thad Mason and Jesse Franklin here. These guys are with the crew too. You might remember Thad, but Jesse's a transplant from Fairbanks."

I said my hellos and looked to Thad. "You were a few years behind me in high school, right?"

Thad nodded and twirled his beer bottle in a circle on the table. "Sure was. Just young enough you guys could ignore me," he said with a chuckle. He had dark brown hair and eyes to match.

Beck took the bait and punched him lightly on the shoulder. "Dude, we weren't ignoring you. We just had eyes for the girls back then. You know how it goes."

I glanced to Levi. "Good to meet you, man. How long have you been with the crew here?"

Levi leaned back in his chair. "About a year. I did my training in Arizona, but I'm from Juneau. When a position opened up here, I jumped on it."

Conversation moved on with me getting updates on everything from the new equipment at the station to Beck's latest ladies drama when he accidentally, according to him, dated two women he hadn't known were friends. I was midway through my second beer when I happened to see the flash of Amelia's hair. Her amber hair glinted gold in the lights from above. Even across the crowded room, I felt her presence like a jolt. I couldn't help but crane my head. The second I did, I regretted it. Earl Osborne was seated across from her.

I saw red and did my damnedest to shackle the irrational jealousy coursing through me. I forced myself to look away, colliding with Beck's too-perceptive gaze. Beck arched a brow, a knowing grin curling one corner of his mouth. I shook my head. Beck's grin faded quickly with a slight nod. Beck might enjoy teasing, but he wasn't an asshole.

A waitress passed by us, and as much as I wanted another beer to bury the jealousy chewing me up inside, I declined. The last thing my anger needed was enough alcohol to make me stupid.

Bar noise hummed around me. I made a strong effort to keep my cool, but it was dicey. I thought I was good enough to get my ass out of there, so I said my goodbyes and stood, tossing a twenty on the table to cover my portion of the tab. I started to make my way through the crowd when my eyes landed on Amelia and Earl. My barely in check jealousy flared when I saw Earl leaning across the table, trying to reach for her hand.

I went from angry to on fire and shouldered my way over to their table. Amelia's eyes whipped to mine. "Come on," I said.

Earl glanced up, his gaze annoyed. "This is none of your business Cade. I know you and Amelia have some history, but..."

Earl made the mistake of reaching for Amelia's hand

again. She drew back, her eyes flashing. "Earl, I already told you. We're done. Period."

"Amelia, you don't get to..."

I grabbed Earl by his shirt, yanking him up out of his chair. No easy feat, given Earl was close to my height and plenty strong. But I was beyond angry. My jealousy was now mixed with raw anger at seeing Earl try to push Amelia on anything. "Fucking listen to her. You don't get to *make* her talk to you anymore."

Earl's eyes were wide now. Whatever he'd thought about us before, realization appeared to be dawning it might be more than old history. "Oh, you think you can just show up in town and call the shots with her? That's fucking bullshit. We were getting married. You're the one who screwed around on her."

I drew back and drove my fist into Earl's face. I didn't hear a damn thing through the fury buzzing like static in my brain. Earl stumbled back. "What the fuck!"

Before Earl had a chance to punch me back, Amelia stepped between us, shoving him to the side. Next thing I knew, Beck was at my side pulling me away. "Back off, man. No one needs this," he murmured, his voice low at my shoulder.

The sounds around me broke through my fury, and I glanced over to see Amelia in Earl's face. I couldn't hear what she was saying, but it was obvious she was pissed. Through the jumble of the next few minutes, Beck dragged me out of the way. Likewise, Earl was pulled out of the way by his brother Dan. I leaned against the wall in the back hallway leading to the restrooms with Beck standing across from me.

"Here's hoping Earl doesn't decide to be more of an ass and press charges," Beck said with a slow shake of his head. "Be great to have your dad dealing with this."

My dad was Willow Brook's chief of police. I knew if Earl decided to be an ass, my dad wouldn't stand in the way.

I loved my dad, but I could count on him not treating me special. I closed my eyes and ran a hand through my hair. "Fuck. Wasn't thinking back there."

Beck chuckled. "Nah, you weren't."

He paused long enough, I opened my eyes.

"So, she's not your girl, huh?" he said with a slow grin.

I leaned my head against the wall and shrugged.

Footsteps sounded in the hallway. I rolled my head to the side to see Amelia walking our way. My heart thudded, and the lust I couldn't seem to turn off around her hit me like a bolt.

She reached us quickly, her long legs eating up the distance between us with ease. Her honey-amber hair fell in tousled waves around her shoulders with her matching eyes glittering bright. Her cheeks were flushed, and she looked, well, the only way to put it was angry. Her cowboy boots struck the hardwood floor, the sound echoing around us as she came to a stop. She wore jeans that hugged her legs, those legs I wanted wrapped around my waist. Atop her jeans, she wore a bright blue silky blouse, unbuttoned over a fitted tank top. My eyes were drawn to the tempting curves of her breasts, and I wanted nothing more than to strip her bare and forget everything else.

It didn't matter that I'd gone and made a mess by punching her very-recent-former fiancé in the middle of everything. I forgot everything but how much I wanted her. Beck's gaze bounced from Amelia to me and back again.

"Well?" Beck asked calmly.

Amelia glanced to him. "Well, what?"

"The obvious—is Earl gonna make this more than it needs to be?"

She shook her head. "Oh you mean press charges? No. He's pissed, but he's not a total ass. I told him he was too pushy with me and needed to back the hell off."

Beck nodded and pushed away from the wall. His eyes

landed on me. "I'm done here. Stay out of trouble for the rest of the night, okay?"

I nodded, swallowing against my frustration at the whole damn mess. Beck strolled down the hallway, leaving us alone there. Amelia looked over at me, her eyes still flashing with anger.

We stood there in the hall, no more than a foot apart. In seconds, the air around us hummed. I had one thing on my mind and that was forgetting the seven years of nothing between us and finally having what I wanted like I'd never wanted anything in my life. I'd had seven years of casual encounters with women and hadn't thought I'd ever want anything more. I also hadn't thought anything could be like what I'd once had with Amelia. What I'd underestimated was the power of seven years of messy feelings swirling into the raw desire I felt for her. It was lust on octane.

Whatever might be passing through her mind, I knew what I felt from her. I reached for her hand, reeling her against me in a flash. She didn't resist, her eyes whipping to mine. I could see the wild beat of her pulse in her neck as her eyes darkened. Her breath came in rough gusts, while my heart thudded so hard, it almost hurt.

"Are you gonna tell me we shouldn't do this?" I asked, my voice coming out gruff.

I knew she could feel my cock, rock hard and nestled right against her core. It was impossible to miss. I'd always loved how we fit together. She was tall enough to meld against me, her curves everywhere I wanted them to be.

She shook her head, just barely. That was all I needed. I tunneled my hand into her hair and fit my mouth over hers. Our kiss went wild instantly with our tongues tangling roughly. I lost sense of anything other than the feel of her against me, pouring my anger, my jealousy and too many years of missing her into our kiss. Footsteps coming our way barely broke through the haze in my brain, but she broke free, her head thudding against the wall behind her.

I hadn't even realized I'd spun us around and pressed her into the wall. One of her boots was curled around my calf as I flexed my hips into the cradle of hers. I could feel her wet heat through the two layers of denim between us. Her eyes locked to mine—wild and dark. She swallowed. "We can't lose it like this here," she whispered.

Chapter Nineteen
AMELIA

I stood there with Cade's cock pressing against my core, sending sharp spikes of pleasure shooting through me. I could barely catch my breath and all I knew was I didn't want this to end. I didn't even care that someone was walking down the hall toward us while I was tangled like a vine around Cade.

Cade's dark green gaze held mine for a beat, and he slowly eased his grip on my hair, his thumb feathering across my pulse as he dragged his hand away. "Well, we could," he replied, his gruff voice sending shivers over my skin. "But as much as I'd love to lose it here in the hallway, let's save it for later. Come on."

He stepped back, instantly leaving me feeling bereft. I missed his heat, his hard muscled body pressing me into the wall, and the feel of his mouth on mine, kissing me as if the world was about to end and the only way to stop it was to kiss me. He curled his hand around mine and tugged me behind him, heading toward the restaurant. Blessedly, I didn't recognize the man walking down the hall and was relieved when he turned into the bathroom. I planted my feet, leading Cade to glance behind him.

"Let's go out the back," I said, gesturing behind me. "There's a door around the corner at the end. After our little scene out there, I'd rather not go that way."

His mouth curled at the corner, one of his devastating, dangerous grins. "Good point."

Heat spiraled through me as he turned and quickly strode the other way. Earl was so far in my rear view mirror, I could hardly believe what I was doing. Tonight was supposed to be a polite dinner with Earl where I explained why I'd broken things off with him—more calmly than I had when I dashed into the rainy afternoon at our not-wedding. I'd underestimated Earl's pride. Not for a second did I believe he wanted me any more than he ever had, but then I doubted he'd ever collided with the pulse-pounding, body-melting desire mingled with shocking intimacy that I felt with Cade. Earl just wasn't the kind of guy to feel much of anything that strongly. He was friendly and comfortable. I didn't wish him ill, but when he'd started to argue the point with me, I realized he didn't get it and thought he had a claim to me.

Before I knew it, Cade had stormed over and lifted Earl out of his chair. I'd like to think I was immune to that brand of alpha masculinity, but I wasn't. At least, not when it came from Cade. He rounded the corner at the end of the hall and shouldered through the door, his hand holding mine firmly as he strode quickly across the parking lot behind the lodge. He stopped abruptly, leading me to collide with him as he turned back to me.

He didn't miss a beat, flashing one of his devastating grins and sliding a hand over my bottom. My breath went shallow the second I felt the heat of his cock against me. "Did you drive here?" he asked, his words a murmur against my lips.

I shook my head. "Uh-uh. I walked from my office."

He held still for a beat, and then spun around again. I'd been expecting a kiss and his tease sent the flames licking inside higher. We were inside his truck in a flash, his hand burning against my thigh as he spun out onto the road.

"Where are we going?" I asked, just when his hand stroked in between my thighs.

If he meant to push them apart, it was entirely unnecessary as my knees parted for him in reflex.

I bit back a moan when he cupped my mound, the subtle pressure against my clit through the denim nearly sending me over the edge. That's how bad I was with him. The moment I let the walls down around everything I felt for him, my control frayed so fast it was ridiculous. It wasn't just about sex with Cade, it never had been. Yet, the chemistry burned so hot, it nearly singed me. Our intimacy fed the fire of desire between us, each notching the other higher.

"Your place," Cade answered as he dragged his thumb across my clit.

I didn't even try to hold back my moan, my hips arching into his touch. "Do you know..."

He came to an abrupt stop at a stop sign, his eyes whipping to mine. I felt branded by his gaze. After a beat, he nodded. "Even when I didn't want to think about you, I did. You still out at the property we looked at before?"

I'd forgotten what it was like to have someone anticipate my thoughts. My heart squeezed and set off on another frenzied bout of pounding. I nodded, wrestling with the emotion coursing through me. Before I stormed out on the heels of that fateful morning, we'd been scouting around for a piece of property to build on when he came back from California. Cade had left town, and I'd held onto my anger as a shield against the hurt and pain. Irrationally, I'd thought I'd go ahead and buy a property we'd loved, thinking I wasn't going to let him take everything from me. I'd built my own home there, determined I wasn't going to let a broken heart stop me. I loved it, but there'd always been a rub, like a grain of sand in my shoe, at the memories of Cade and the dreams we once had.

After my nod, Cade spun his truck onto the highway, heading in the direction of my home. Minutes later—taut with his hand teasing me so subtly I thought I might explode—he turned onto the road leading to my cabin. It was still light out, even though it was approaching 11pm. Summer evenings in Alaska were a long, slow dance with dusk. Darkness would fall soon, but not quite yet.

He slowed, glancing to me. "You'll have to show me where your drive is," he said, his voice low and taut and threaded with a hint of uncertainty.

In a flash, I realized he was as much of a mess as I was. When we'd looked at this land back then, it had been empty —no driveway, nothing to mark it. Realizing he'd never actually been to my place was like a knife slicing across my heart —a sharp sting of pain right where it hurt the most. We'd missed so much and all over a very well-timed manipulation. I caught his gaze and gestured to a drive just ahead.

Cade turned into the driveway and slowed, his eyes scanning the area. My cabin was in a wooded area, a mix of blue spruce with clusters of cottonwood and birch scattered here and there. There were other homes nearby now, although not within sight. The trees opened up onto a small field with a shallow pond over to one side. My driveway curved in a circle at the end. He rolled his truck to a stop and slowly drew his hand away. Though I was so turned on I was about to melt into a puddle, I sensed the intensity of his emotion.

I climbed out along with him and went to stand at his side. In the smudgy light of late dusk, the pond looked magical with the rising moon coming up behind the trees and casting a silvery glow over everything. He looked out over the field and turned to look at the cabin.

"You built this?" he asked.

Wordlessly, I nodded. I didn't quite know what to do with the emotions thundering through me. Somehow, this felt more momentous than I'd anticipated. Having him here in this place we'd once intended to share felt so enormous, it crashed over me.

I followed his eyes to the cabin. It was the first project I'd completed entirely on my own. It was a smallish cabin, nestled into the edge of the trees with the small field and pond to the other side. There were decks on both floors with the one upstairs a small curved deck, mimicking the larger curve of the deck on the lower floor.

Cade was quiet, so quiet I started to get anxious. He reached for my hand and walked to the cabin. We climbed the stairs together, every step feeling monumental. I didn't lock my door because it was unnecessary. We stepped through, the door falling closed behind us on a whisper. My cabin had a shared living room and kitchen in most of the downstairs with a bathroom and laundry area to the back. An open loft upstairs led to the bedroom and another bathroom.

His eyes scanned the space, while my heart pounded a wild, frantic beat. Restless, I started to pull free, but he tightened his grip on my hand.

"Don't."

His word fell into the quiet, his voice husky and sending a prickle up my spine. I looked over at him, instantly caught in his gaze. He reeled me to him. My body remembered his and came flush against him, as if it had been just yesterday that we slept together every night. Oh God. He felt so good. So hard, so strong, so everything I wanted because he was Cade, the only man I'd ever been able to let go with.

"It's nice," he whispered.

My confusion must've shown because his mouth curled at one corner. "This place. I like it," he added.

I swallowed and nodded. I couldn't really talk, not with my pulse running wildly, heat suffusing me, and my longing for him so profound, I couldn't think past any of it.

He lifted his hand, sifting his fingers through my hair. "It really pissed me off to see you with Earl."

"I wasn't *with* him the way you mean."

I felt his shrug, his low chuckle vibrating through my body.

"It didn't matter to me."

His words encircled my heart. The implied jealousy made me flush, inside and out. I'd forgotten how it felt to be wanted this way.

"I was never with him the way I am with you. Never with anyone."

His gaze darkened as his hand slid into my hair to cup my nape, his thumb brushing in a maddening tease along the side of my neck.

"That's good to know. Because for me, it's always been you."

We stood like that, flush against each other in the center of the room with the silvery moonlight cast through the windows. I could barely breathe with fierce need radiating through me. His voice startled me. I'd sunk into the quiet, into the heartbeat of nothing but sensation and desire thrumming between us.

"I don't think I can go slow," he said.

A hot shiver raced through me, want coiling tighter in my core. I could feel the wetness between my thighs and knew I was soaked for him. "I don't think I can either," I finally managed to say, my voice coming out raspy.

At that, his eyes darkened further. In a flash, his mouth was on mine and he was tugging at my clothes. There was no slow build up. I was so fraught with need, I'd have lost my mind if he weren't matching my madness. As it was, clothes were torn off and strewn about as we stumbled across the room.

I managed to flick on a lamp by the couch when Cade paused to kick his shoes off after he almost fell over when I shoved his jeans down. I tumbled to the couch, bare except for my blue silk panties, the one article of clothing where my streak of femininity showed. His remaining boot thumped to the floor behind him, and he kicked his jeans free. I looked up at him, and my mouth went dry. Oh. My. God.

It wasn't that I didn't know what he looked like. I'd even had a chance to get my hands on him once recently. But it had been a long seven years since I'd seen him fully naked. He'd gone from a sexy as hell young man to a hard, muscled, dangerously sexy man. I knew his job was about as physically demanding as it could get, but still. There wasn't an inch of him that wasn't honed and hard. He had a dusting of dark hair on his chest, his skin glinting amber in the soft light.

He looked down at me, his eyes dark and intent. Everywhere his eyes landed lit small fires under my skin. He leaned over and dragged his finger across the silk between my thighs. "You're so fucking wet."

I couldn't even speak, but my hips rolled into his touch. I cried out when he drew away. He wasted no time and hooked a finger over the edge of my panties, dragging them off roughly and tossing them aside. He leaned over to snag his jeans off the floor. Puzzled, I shook my head when I realized he was tugging a condom out of his wallet.

"I'm on the pill, and I'm clean. Except for you..." I had to pause when emotion choked me. Aside from him, I'd never had sex with anyone without a condom. Cade was the man I'd lost my virginity to and the man who'd gone with me when I went to the doctor to start taking the pill. When I tried dating again, I simply couldn't bring myself to let anyone past that layer. Not even Earl, not even when I thought I was going to marry him.

When Cade was silent, his hand frozen midair with a condom packet held in it, I got anxious. "Unless, I mean... Maybe..."

Whatever he saw in my eyes snapped him into motion. He tossed the condom packet to the floor and stretched out over me quickly. I hadn't realized a tear had rolled down my cheek until he wiped it away with his thumb. It was such a relief to have him against me, his weight and strength wrapping me into the moment with him. His cock rested against my slick folds and need clawed at me, but I had to catch my breath.

He dusted kisses over my face. "God, Lia. Don't look like that. I can't take it," he murmured.

"Well, I didn't know what you were thinking," I managed, gasping when his hips rocked against me, his cock sliding over my clit.

"It's been seven years since I had sex with anyone without a condom, so I was just a little startled. Don't think for a second I don't want it," he said, his hips arching into me again.

I took a shuddering breath, trying and failing to corral the wild need pounding through me. I didn't want to talk anymore. "Cade, please..." Whatever I'd meant to say got lost the second he drew back and surged inside of me.

He curled his hands into mine, stretching them above my head. His eyes were like hot embers on me. I felt the burn of his gaze and couldn't look away. He held still for a moment, and I sighed at the feel of my channel stretching to accommodate him. It felt so good, so right to have him filling me. I could feel his heart pounding in time with mine, his skin hot and slick against me. After a moment, he began to move. My sex clenched around him as he stroked into me—long and deep, he drove into me again and again and again. There was nothing gentle about this—my legs curled around him, my hips colliding with the rough pounding of his, his hands tightening their grip on mine, the scrape of his teeth against my neck and the burn of his eyes when I started to unravel.

Pleasure ripped through me, my climax so intense, I spun loose inside. The only thing anchoring me was the feel of Cade against me. He let out a growl, my name following in a rough cry as he went taut and then collapsed against me.

Chapter Twenty
CADE

I opened my eyes, momentarily disoriented. I wasn't accustomed to waking to the feel of soft curves against me. Through the haze of sleep, I remembered it was Amelia sleeping beside me. The tension that had started to build inside eased instantly. I was on my back with one of her legs thrown across mine and her foot tucked in between my calves. My heart clenched at the familiar feel of her. I eased up on the pillows and glanced down at her. Her amber hair was a tousled mess around her face and shoulders. Emotion rocked me, colliding with the lust setting fire in my veins.

There'd never been any shortage of chemistry between us, yet somehow seven years mixed with a tangle of pain, regret and anger was like pouring octane fuel on the fire burning between us. I sifted my fingers through her hair, idly untangling the silky strands. She shifted slightly in her sleep, the feel of her skin sliding against mine sending blood straight to my groin. I wanted to savor this moment—the simple act of waking up with the one and only woman I'd ever loved on the heels of years of thinking we'd never have this chance again was so good I didn't want to miss it. Yet, my body wasn't so interested in taking anything slow. My need for her went from sleepy arousal to burning need so fast, it was hard to keep a grip.

When we'd made our way up here last night, we'd showered, and despite the fact I'd just spent myself inside of her once, one look at the water sluicing over her had me sliding my hands over her bottom and reaching between her thighs to find her hot, wet and ready. In a flash, I sank into her clenching heat.

After that, we'd tumbled into bed in the darkness. I took a slow breath and rolled my head to the side, glancing out the windows. She'd wisely situated the small home such that the windows to the front offered a clear view of the adjacent field and pond. In the early morning light, mist rose off the water. A flock of sandhill cranes was pecking at the grass at the edge of the field. Knowing Amelia, I'd guess she tossed cracked corn out for them all summer long. Sandhill cranes migrated to Alaska every summer and typically returned to the same area year after year. The tall, leggy birds could easily blend into the grass, but for their bright red crowns atop their heads. This flock had likely been coming here long before Amelia built here, yet she'd have gone out of her way to make sure her presence didn't scare them away.

I took a steadying breath, trying to contain the emotion and need coursing through me. Amelia was a bundle of soft, lush curves against me. She shifted again, and I nearly groaned aloud. I felt her come awake with a subtle thread of tension humming through her body. She lifted her head, her amber eyes catching mine. God, I loved how she looked when she was sleepy. By nature, she was a strong, bold, confident woman. It was rare to see her with her guard down, but when she was sleepy it was. She stared at me, completely quiet for a moment, but I felt her heart starting to thud against me.

"Mornin'," I said, brushing a few tangled strands of hair away from her eyes.

Her cheeks flushed. "Good morning. Um..."

Her words trailed off, and she glanced away, starting to look like she was thinking way too much.

"Amelia?"

Her eyes whipped back to mine.

"Don't."

"Don't what?"

"Start thinking too much."

She stiffened, and I couldn't help but grin. I'd forgotten how much I enjoyed getting under her skin, even just a little.

"I'm not..."

I moved fast, lifting her up and over me. She gasped, but she didn't resist, which might've been fun. Her knees landed on either side of my hips. Exactly where I wanted her.

I looked up at her. The early morning sun was falling through the windows at an angle, catching her hair in its light and glinting it with gold. I could feel her slick heat against me. I was tempted, so fucking tempted, to drive into her right now. I couldn't help it and arched into her. She gasped and closed her eyes.

"Wait. Not yet," I bit out.

Her eyes flew open, lasering me with a glare.

"Don't you dare tease like that," she said, her voice still rough from sleep.

She started to rise up, but I was ready and I knew what I wanted.

In a flash, I rolled us and stretched out over her. There were so many things I wanted—perhaps a full week in bed with her would give me enough time—but right now, I had to taste her. I mapped my way down her body with my hands and lips, pausing to dally over her breasts. Full and round with taut, pink nipples, I could've spent all day there.

If she was still annoyed with me, it was lost amidst her rough sighs and occasional moans. I spread her knees apart, trailing my fingers up the insides of her thighs, which earned me a murmured curse. I dragged a finger through her folds.

She was so wet, her thighs were damp. I meant to take my time, but the lust pounding through me was so strong, I couldn't. I sank a finger knuckle-deep, savoring the clenching of her channel. A dip of my head and I set to exploring her with my tongue, while I fucked her with my fingers.

She tasted so good, I settled in—licking, stroking and sucking. I meant to make her come apart, but I'd forgotten how demanding she could be. She gripped my hair and yanked. I lifted my head, still toying inside her with my fingers, stretching and stroking.

"I need you. Now," she demanded, her voice rough and raspy.

"You have me," I countered, enjoying her frustration.

With her sex clenching around me, I drew my thumb in a slow circle around her clit.

Her head fell back on a throaty cry, but she was only momentarily deterred. She lifted her head. Damn. She was fucking glorious with her hair a tangle around her face, her skin flushed and damp, and her breasts rising and falling with her heavy pants.

"Inside," she ordered.

I dragged my fingers out and sank them in deep. "Like this?"

She muttered a curse and yanked at me. Seeing as I wanted the same thing, I stopped teasing. The moment I was stretched atop her, our bodies flush together and the tip of my cock at her entrance, I held still, locking eyes with her. Electricity fairly snapped in the air around us. The intensity of connection I felt with her—so sharp it pierced my heart—hit me with a force so strong, I lost my breath. I stared at her—hard—and slowly sank into her. Again, what I meant to do and what happened weren't the same. I wanted to go slow, to be able to savor every millisecond of this, but my body was having none of that. The forces driving within us, between us and around us were so powerful, the moment I sank into her creamy clench, raw, primal instinct took over.

Her legs curled around my hips, her nails scored my back, and I drummed into her, every stroke deeper than the last. I felt the shudder roll through her body, her channel pulsing around my cock. She cried out, my name a rough shout, just as my own release thundered through me. I fell against her, annihilated inside and out by the release and what it felt like to be with her. As my breath slowly eased and my heart stopped pounding so hard I could barely hear, I shifted my weight to her side.

We lay in a sweaty tangle. After a moment, I felt her eyes on me and opened mine. Her eyes were clear. After a beat, she reached up and smoothed my brows with her fingertip.

Chapter Twenty-One

AMELIA

I leaned my elbows on the counter and watched as Cade practically inhaled the omelet I'd served him a few minutes ago. I'd managed to get through most of the morning without letting my pushy, critical mind get in the way of the best morning I'd had in as long as I could remember. Last night had been amazing. This morning had been amazing. It felt so strange and familiar at once to be with Cade like this again. It was hard to believe the ugly part of last night had even happened. I still didn't know quite what to think of how easily I'd let go of Earl. In hindsight, it was brutally clear I'd never loved him. My mind and heart were filled with Cade and Cade alone.

I wasn't in the mood to avoid anything anymore. I'd wasted two years of my life on Earl and far more all because I'd been so good at avoiding anything that made me think about Cade. Funny thing was, despite my stubborn, herculean efforts, Cade had never been far from my mind. All I'd succeeded at was blocking myself from the truth. What a waste.

The coffee maker beeped and I turned to check it. After

filling two mugs, I slid one across the counter and sat down across from him. "So, when did you say you start work?"

"Monday," he said between bites.

"What are you doing today?"

He took a slow sip of coffee, his green gaze assessing. "Whatever you're doing," he said, a slow grin curling the corners of his mouth.

I smiled straight through to my toes, emotion rocking me as tears pricked at my eyes.

His smile faded, and he set his coffee down, reaching over to curl his hand around mine. "Hey, if it's too much, just say so. There's what I want now and what I want long-term. I don't want to take it slow, but I know maybe the timing's not the best." He paused, his throat working and his eyes locking to mine—his intent gaze making me feel as if he could see right into my heart. "I don't want to fuck this up again."

I swallowed against the emotion clogging my throat and shook my head. "It's not that. It's just everything feels so good and I'm so glad you're here and I just don't want to mess up. As far as I'm concerned, you should just stay right here and never leave."

He chuckled, the low rumble curling around my heart. "Well, that's easy. As it is, I'm shacking up with my parents until I find somewhere else. Trust me, my mom'll do a dance if I tell her I'm staying with you."

"She probably would." I paused to sip my coffee. "I think I should feel bad about Earl, but I don't. I walked out on us before I even knew you were coming home. And all the reasons I did were because it had never been right."

I chewed on the inside of my cheek and looked over at Cade. He took another bite of his omelet. After he finished chewing, he eyed me and shrugged. "Honestly, I'm not thinking so much about Earl, but us. If taking things slow means we don't screw this six ways to Sunday again, I'll do it."

I took another sip of coffee, savoring the bitter flavor and pondering how to say what I knew needed to be said. "We might have done things differently, but Shannon's the one who lied."

Darkness flashed in Cade's eyes. "It's fair to say we're both pretty stubborn," he finally said.

I squeezed his hand. "Maybe. Tell me, are you still mad at me?"

He arched a brow in question.

"For getting so angry I never gave you a chance to explain," I added.

He squeezed my hand in return and took a swallow of coffee, his eyes considering. "I was, but I'm not now. Look, I don't blame you for a second for getting pissed that morning. Hell, I couldn't even deal with you sitting at a table with Earl even when I knew why you were there." He paused and set his coffee down, reaching for my other hand and holding both in his. "We can't change the past. I came home prepared to get used to living without you when I knew you were nearby. It was fucking hell when I was over three thousand miles away, but I didn't have to see you. Then, well, everything changed and now we're here. Let's just take it one day at a time. If there's one thing you don't need to worry about it's me going anywhere and wanting anyone else. Hell, I missed you so damn much, I didn't even bother trying to find someone else."

"You didn't see anyone? At all?" I asked. I couldn't help the tiny swirls of doubts in my mind. The old seeds of insecurity planted by Shannon's manipulation and the reality most guys just didn't know how to deal with me were hard to move beyond. It wasn't like I went around thinking I was an ugly duckling. No, rather I knew quite well most men preferred women who didn't stand eye to eye with them. It was what it was. I'd never bothered with the bigger implications of that and what it said about the world we lived in. I stared over at him.

He gave my hands a squeeze before freeing one to snag his coffee cup and take a long swallow. "I wasn't celibate if that's what you're asking, but I haven't slept beside anyone since you."

His eyes held mine, and my heart set to hammering so hard and fast I could barely breathe as the enormity of what he meant sank in. I'd thought I was alone in my complete acceptance that no one else would ever measure up to what I had with Cade.

Chapter Twenty-Two
CADE

I walked into the fire station and leaned my elbows on the reception desk. Maisie was on the phone, her eyes flicking to me as if puzzled at my presence. It was midway through my second week on duty, and I'd determined I was going to kill her with kindness. It just goes to show how prickly she was that me, a man who'd worn my bitterness toward women like a badge for years, was trying to cajole her into being nicer.

But damn. She was like a cactus, and Carol had been more like a mother hen to all of us. It was difficult to believe Maisie was actually related to her. They shared the same wide brown eyes, and though my memories of Carol when she was younger were through the hazy lens of a little boy, I recalled her being pretty. Maisie could be if she stopped glaring at everyone.

I'd mentioned to Amelia that I missed Carol and couldn't quite believe Carol had persuaded my father to agree to hire Maisie for dispatch. She'd looked over at me and sighed, reminding me Maisie had spent her childhood dragged all over the place with pretty much nowhere to call home.

According to Amelia, Maisie had come to visit Carol when she was in hospice, and Carol had asked my father to give her a chance with a job. She'd then pointedly ordered me to be nice.

I figured if Maisie couldn't pamper me and the guys, we'd kill her with kindness. In my short time here, I watched her ignore all the guys, studiously avoid anything resembling a friendly conversation and wear the chip on her shoulder as if it were a cinder block. She'd been so prickly, the rest of the guys avoided her at all costs with the exception of Beck who occasionally, very occasionally, eyed her and made some attempt at small talk. Beck's exterior was like a non-stick pan—everything slid right off of him, so Maisie's unfriendliness didn't bother him much.

All in all, I was feeling magnanimous. The last two weeks had been about the best of my life. Being with Amelia was just short of heaven. Oh, we had some stuff to get through, and she was as stubborn as I remembered, but then so was I. The best thing about arguments was we knew how to have fucking awesome makeup sex. My libido, long sidelined to casual encounters, was getting a hell of a workout these days. Only an hour ago, Amelia's mouth had been wrapped around my cock in the shower. That was after I'd been buried to the hilt inside of her right after we woke up.

There was my overall good mood and the fact I preferred to have my crew like and trust our main dispatcher. I didn't worry Maisie wouldn't be on the dot when it came to her job. She took it very seriously. Her attitude, however, left more than a little to be desired.

I leaned on my elbows and smiled at her when she finally tapped to end whatever call she was on. She adjusted her headset and glared up at me. "Can I help you?" she said stiffly.

She had no idea how lucky she was I wasn't feeling as cranky as I had been for seven years straight. Otherwise, I'd have snapped right back at her. Instead, I reminded myself to be patient. If I didn't want her to act like this, I needed to not be an asshole.

"Rex, Beck and I were hoping to have lunch with you," I said. Beck and I had chatted with my father the other day about doing this.

Maisie raised one of her dark brows, staring at me as if I'd just proposed she go roll in a puddle of mud.

"Why?" was her only reply.

"Because you're our main dispatcher, and we'd like to meet to talk about a few things around the station."

I heard the door open and close behind me. Glancing over my shoulder, I saw Beck approaching. Beck leaned against the counter beside me, his eyes flicking from me to Maisie. Beck ran a hand through his black curls. "Well, I see you're as friendly as usual," he said to Maisie.

Maisie's cheeks flared red. If possible, I was fairly certain her eyes would have burned holes in Beck. She huffed and crossed her arms. "I don't have to be friendly. I take my job seriously and all calls are routed promptly."

Beck eyed her, and I sensed a thread of irritation from him. Not unusual given how flat-out cranky Maisie was, but unusual for Beck. After a beat, Beck glanced to me and nodded as if he expected me to handle her.

I had trained for all kinds of things as a hotshot firefighter and had been foreman on a crew in California for three years. None of that prepared me for an epically cranky dispatcher who had my crew running for cover whenever they happened to be near her.

"Maisie, let me rephrase. We're going to lunch. You're coming with us. This is not a request. Consider it a job meeting. I've already arranged coverage. Meet us here at noon," I said.

Her eyes widened, and her mouth tightened, but she nodded without a word. I pushed away from the counter and strode through the door into the back.

Beck followed me. The moment we made it to the break

room in back and saw no one was around, Beck rolled his eyes. "Damn. That woman can be a serious bitch. Gotta say, I'm glad you're here. She's only been with us a few months, and I've been so damn busy covering both crews, I didn't have time to notice how she was affecting the guys. Plus, your dad's pretty protective of her."

I caught the back of a chair at the break table and swung it out to sit down. Beck plunked down across from me with a sigh.

I chuckled. "Yeah, she's not easy. Practically the opposite of her grandmother."

I glanced behind him to the counter lining the wall, eying the coffee pot. Seeing it was half full, I stood and grabbed a mug. "Want some?" I asked, glancing to Beck as I poured. At Beck's nod, I passed the first mug to him and filled another for myself before sitting back down.

"I'd bet my dad's protective of her. You know him. He's a softie. Carol was one of my mom's good friends too, so she probably sweet-talked him into hiring Maisie."

Beck took a gulp of coffee and leaned back in his chair. "Oh, I'm sure of it. Honestly, if we can get her to just be neutral, it's a win. She does a good job. She's fast and actually good on the line with the emergency calls. She's sharp and focused, which keeps her from getting sidetracked by being freaked out. She also doesn't laugh when people call about the craziest shit. Did you hear about the guy who called because someone was trying to relocate his hunting cabin?"

I almost spit out my coffee. "What?!"

Beck nodded with a gleam in his eyes. "Oh yeah. Only in Alaska. Guy has a cabin out toward the mountains for hunting. Calls up and says someone has the place up on jacks to load onto a trailer. I mean, it was a small place, but still. Fuckin' hilarious! Anyway, I'd have laughed my ass off if I took that call. Maisie stayed cool the whole way through. Good thing too because the guy was seriously pissed. So your dad headed out there and then called us for help to get the cabin back onto its pilings. A change of pace for us, that's for sure."

I shook my head. "Change of pace is one way to put it. What the hell did my dad charge the attempted cabin thief with?"

"Attempted theft," Beck said with a shrug. "He put a dollar figure on it, but the guy who owned the cabin thought it wasn't enough. You know how that goes. Anyway, rumor has it you're shacked up with your girl again."

I couldn't help it. Just thinking I could actually call Amelia my girl again made me feel so damn good. I flashed a wry grin. "Rumor may be true."

I'd been staying at her place every night since the first night I'd been there. I sobered. "Seriously, I'm guessing Earl might have some thoughts about that, but... Hell, I don't know. It's like we picked up right where we left off."

"Doesn't really matter what Earl thinks. Plenty of chatter about it, but who gives a damn? Look, Earl's not a bad guy, but he's always been a tad too sure of himself for me. Look at me, I play the field and like it that way. Earl's always done the same, but tries to act like he doesn't. Amelia was like a prize for him. You're damn lucky he didn't make the other night into more than it was. He's like that. Kinda petty if you ask me."

I couldn't help but wonder what Amelia had ever seen in him. Then, I remembered what she'd said—something to the effect that was the best she'd get. Just like that, I felt as if I'd been kicked in the gut. Though we were floating along in a hazy, lust-driven madness after seven years apart, I knew there were some deep waters getting stirred. I had my own anger I'd clung to after she shut me out, while I knew she had her own pain after seeing Shannon make a play for me. I didn't want either one of those issues to linger in any way. I hated the rub of worrying about her thinking she didn't deserve more.

I was about to reply when the intercom crackled and

Maisie announced a call for a fire downtown. Within minutes, the rest of the local crew was buzzing through the station and sirens were blaring as they flew down to respond.

Chapter Twenty-Three
AMELIA

I stood beside Lucy and scanned the lot in front of us. As promised, Max had arrived last week and taken care of the excavation. It was early evening now, and the foundation crew had left for the day. I took care of the architectural design for projects, while Lucy and I handled the construction together. I contracted out for excavation, foundation work, and plumbing. Conveniently, Lucy was also a certified electrician.

I grinned when I met Lucy's eyes. "Time to start building."

Lucy held her hand aloft for a high-five. "You got it," she said when our hands collided with a whack. "Should we start tonight or wait until tomorrow?"

Alaskan summers created an odd dynamic. On the one hand, when it came to anything one might want to do outdoors, summer felt so short. Yet, on the other hand, the days were so long, the hours added up to about the same as a longer summer. My construction business felt like a race every year. Long days, short nights, and every project I felt I could handle crammed in.

I considered Lucy's question. Since it was after seven in the evening, we could knock out a few hours of work right now if we wanted before darkness rolled in. If it weren't for Cade, I probably would've said yes. I caught Lucy's eyes and shook my head. "Nah. Let's start tomorrow. Meet at seven?"

Lucy's eyes crinkled at the corner with her sly grin. "You seem to have changed your work habits lately."

I fought to keep from flushing, but my cheeks heated against my will. "Maybe. You got a problem with that?"

Lucy shook her head. "Nope. You're the boss. You haven't said much, but I'm guessing things are pretty darn okay with Cade."

My cheeks got even hotter. "Things are..." I paused when I realized I was about to say 'great.' Because that's how it felt. Actually, great didn't even capture how good it felt to have Cade home with me again. I felt as if I'd been alone in the desert for years. He'd been a mirage in my memory for so long, and now he was real—everything I remembered and more. Just as I imagined, he'd grown and settled into himself. He was all man and he was mine again. Yet, there was a tiny corner of my mind that worried I was diving in too fast after walking out on Earl. It had only been a month ago that I'd been an hour before my not-wedding.

I thanked my stars time and again that I'd had enough sense to make my choice about Earl before I saw Cade, before I had any clue he was moving home. Otherwise, I'd be even more of a mess over it all. As it was, I was so far gone over Cade, if he proposed we get married tonight, I wouldn't even hesitate. And that scared the hell out of me. I'd pretty much fallen apart inside over him before. I didn't know if I was up for being this vulnerable again. But that was the problem when it came to me with Cade—I was always vulnerable. He meant too much. We meant too much.

I glanced back to Lucy. "Things are pretty darn okay with Cade."

Lucy flashed a grin and started to walk toward the work

truck parked at the edge of the lot. I walked alongside her. When we reached the truck, Lucy hooked her arm on the back and eyed me. "As relaxed as you've been, I'd bet you two have almost burned your cabin down a few times."

I burst out laughing. When I caught my breath, I shrugged. "Maybe so. He's a firefighter though, so we'll be fine."

Lucy's grin faded, her gaze becoming somber. "Just checking in, but you were, well, a little stressed about him before. I'm sure the sex is great, and trust me, I see how he looks at you, but have you sorted out all the mess from before?"

I eyed her for a long moment and nodded. "I think so. I mean, it was a giant misunderstanding. Made worse by me being stubborn as hell and him being gone the whole time."

Lucy laughed softly. "You're definitely stubborn as hell. Just making sure you're okay."

I sensed something was up. Lucy wasn't one to over-worry. "What's up?"

"Just checking because I heard from Janet that Shannon's back. Because she heard Cade was back in town," Lucy said flatly.

My gut started churning. The pain of walking in on Shannon climbing in bed naked with Cade was scabbed over, but still there. I tried to remind myself Cade had told me the truth, but my emotions on the matter weren't exactly sensible. "What the fuck is she doing here? Doesn't she live in Anchorage now?"

Lucy nodded. "Far as I know, but it's not like she can't come up with some excuse to visit. Her sister's still around. Look, I just want you to be okay. You and Cade are pretty fresh. I wasn't sure if I should give you a heads up, but, well, now I did. Her showing up like this doesn't mean anything. You and Cade are together, and good God that man practically drools when he's around you. Just be prepared if you run into her."

I kicked my boot against one of the tires, beating back that old feeling of betrayal and all the insecurity that came with it. "This is bullshit. Why would she do this? I mean, he chased her off last time. He's been gone for seven years. Does she hate me that much? I mean, we're back together..."

Lucy cut in. "I don't think she knows that. I realize it might seem like forever ago, but you *were* supposed to get married to Earl only a month ago. Janet said she didn't think Shannon knew what was up. You have to realize she pissed a lot of people off over what she pulled. I wasn't close to you then, but it was impossible not to hear how angry people were with her. No matter what anyone thought of you and Cade, she pulled a hardcore bitch move. Now you know. Watch your back. You might want to give lover boy a heads up too."

I was too angry to laugh. My misery must've shown on my face. Lucy stepped to me and pulled me into a fierce hug. For a small person, Lucy's hugs were powerful. She threw her arms around my shoulders and gave me a hard squeeze before bouncing away. "I'll kick her ass if she tries anything. And remember, you and Cade are solid. Now go home and screw his brains out."

Chapter Twenty-Four
CADE

I stood under the hot water, my hands resting against the tiles and my head bowed. The fire this afternoon had gone from bad to worse, necessitating back up support from my crew for the local crew after the hotel beside the house on fire was threatened. The fire had started after the homeowner left the coffee pot on when they left the house. The house was a total loss, but we'd managed to keep the fire from spreading to the hotel. With the hotel adjacent to a swath of spruce forest, it was a damn good thing.

It was high summer in Alaska with not enough rain and acres and acres of spruce forest filled with spruce trees dead or dying from spruce bark beetle. As such, the already problematic fire conditions that were getting worse with every dry summer out West were made much worse with so much dead, dry fuel. Blue spruce trees were hardier and more able to resist the beetles, but flying overhead, sometimes my heart cracked. We'd fly for miles and see nothing but brown, dead swaths of spruce trees. Keeping that section of forest from catching fire was a lucky break.

I'd had a long afternoon and was tired as hell. I'd come to

know Amelia tended to work late in the evenings. No surprise, so when I arrived at her cabin to find her gone, I headed straight for a shower. I stood there and let the hot water pound down on me. I heard a soft click and glanced over my shoulder to find Amelia stepping into the shower with me. I let my hands fall and turned to face her. The second my body knew she was near, my cock swelled. By the time I was facing her, I was rock hard and ready. She was untangling her hair from a messy ponytail. She had a streak of dirt on her cheek and one on her arm. My eyes traveled over her—savoring the contrast of her strong legs and lush breasts.

"Dammit," she muttered as she glanced over at me.

She couldn't miss the fact I was fully erect, her eyes widening slowly with a naughty grin curling the corner of her mouth.

I stepped to her, satisfaction rolling through me when her breath drew in sharply as I came flush against her. "Dammit, what?" I murmured, my lips feathering against her neck.

"I can't get this thing out of my hair," she said between gasps.

I lifted my head, reaching up to help her. She dropped her hands. It took a minute, but I managed to get the elastic out and let it fall to the floor. "There," I said, my voice coming out rough when I met her eyes and saw them darkening.

"How was your day?" she whispered.

"Busy. Yours?" I returned as I slid my hands down to cup her bottom.

Another gasp from her when I pulled her tight against me. I bit back a groan at the feel of her heated core against my cock.

When she didn't answer me, I repeated my question in between licks and nips along her neck. "Your day? How was it?" I murmured.

"Oh God, it was fine," she muttered as she curled her hand around my cock and stroked.

Steam cocooned us as the water fell around us. She felt so fucking good, slick and wet all over. I reached between her thighs and found her hot, wet and ready. I wasn't in the mood to wait. I hooked my hands under her thighs and lifted her, pressing her back against the tiled wall.

She curled her legs around my hips as her head thumped against the wall. I had my cock in my fist about to sink inside of her when I looked at her. My heart gave a resounding kick. Her hair was a damp, tangled mess, her eyes like molten honey, her nipples pink and taut, and her breasts so full and round. I loved the sight of her, loved everything about her. So much it almost hurt.

She rolled her hips as she bit her lip. I adjusted her where I held her with one arm hooked firmly under her hips and nudged into the cradle of her hips, lifting my hand and brushing the damp strands of hair away from her face. I traced her lips with my thumb. Her eyes darkened, and she caught my thumb in her teeth, drawing it in to suck on it lightly.

"I love you," I said, the words burning fiercely inside and coming out rough.

In the pulse of the moment, I felt her tense. Her eyes took on a sheen and a tear slipped out one corner. It wasn't that I hadn't known I loved her, forever it felt like. But I hadn't spoken the words aloud in seven years. I waited, wondering if I'd said too much, too soon. I drew my thumb out of her mouth and trailed my fingers down her neck, across the wild flutter of her pulse.

"I love you too," she finally said, waiting just long enough I thought I might die from it.

"Okay then," I managed.

Words were a poor substitute for everything I felt, so I used my body. I eased my hips back slightly, adjusted my angle and slid home in one swift surge. She cried out and tightened her legs around my hips. With my eyes locked to hers, I held her with the water pounding down around us and poured everything I felt into the beat of the desire that lived and breathed between us as its own force.

Every stroke brought me deeper, every raw groan from me and rough cry from her, every slap of our wet skin, all of it was more than words could ever say. In the heat of this frantic, wet coupling, we were rough and wild, but underneath was the fierce tenderness that bound us together— that which we'd lost sight of before. I felt her tightening, shudders rippling through her. I sank again and again and again into her creamy clench until I felt her throbbing around me. Her nails scored my back when she cried out. I followed her over, my own release thundering through me with such force, my knees almost gave out.

But she was there, her hands sliding up to cup my cheeks, murmuring my name and feathering kisses over my face. We stayed like that, my cock buried deep inside of her, my lips against hers and hot water streaming over us, for so long the water started to cool.

Chapter Twenty-Five
AMELIA

I pushed through the door into the Firehouse Café and gave my raincoat a shake once I was inside. The morning had dawned gray and rainy, and the rain hadn't let up all day. Lucy and I had finally decided to call it quits early after pushing through some work in the chilly rain for a few hours. I pushed my hood back and glanced around. The café was crowded with tourists, which figured. Any planned fishing trips on the lake or to nearby rivers had likely been cancelled, along with any other outdoor activities. The hard-core eco-tourists wouldn't blink at rain like this, but those were the ones who took off on weeklong backcountry hikes, the kind my brother used to lead with his wife. The tourists who crowded the streets of Willow Brook and the highways of Alaska with their campers usually preferred the wilderness when it was comfortable. Even during the warmest time of year in Alaska, rain meant chilly days.

I wove through the tables and joined the line to the counter, leaning against one of the old fire poles decorated with painted fireweed. My mind spun to last night when Cade had brought me to tears in the shower before making love to me so fiercely. In spite of my memories of what we had before, I hadn't recalled the intensity, the fierce tenderness and a feeling of intimacy so deep it shook me to my core. Maybe it was because we'd lost each other. Maybe it was because the loss and regret coloring the present made it that much more precious. Whatever it is, it felt so good, it was overwhelming.

The line inched forward. Lost in my thoughts, I jumped when I heard my name. I glanced over my shoulder to find Earl standing behind me. When I'd seen him the other night, I'd expected to feel something. But then I should've known better. All I felt was a gentle sense of sadness. I felt genuinely bad things had played out the way they did, but nothing other than that. He stood there with his blondish-brown hair and brown eyes. Objectively speaking, he was a handsome man. At the moment, I couldn't even believe I'd ever tried to date him, much less agreed to marry him. My body's response to him was, at best, lukewarm.

I aimed for casual and friendly, well aware that the last time I'd seen Earl, Cade had ended up punching him. Whatever bruising there had been had faded in the weeks since. "Hey Earl, how's it going?"

His gaze was considering. After a beat, he shrugged. "Fine as I can be after everything."

The line inched forward. I felt a flash of guilt, but I didn't know what to do with it. I wondered if now was the time to say anything, but no one was paying attention, and the hum of conversation in the café drowned out individual conversations.

"Earl, I meant what I said the other night. I'm sorry about all of it. I don't expect you to admit it, but I know you weren't crushed by what happened. Your ego is bruised maybe, but I know what love is and we didn't have it. I'm more sorry than you know it took me as long as it did to think about what that meant for us. I wish you the best and I hope you find what you want."

Earl looked away, staring at the chalkboard above the counter where Janet was rapidly taking orders and entering them in the computer. "I hear you and Cade are back together," he said, his tone flat.

My stomach fluttered. Hearing it out loud like that made it oddly real. I beat back my response. The last thing Earl needed was me looking all gooey-eyed and silly over Cade. When he glanced to me, I nodded. "We are. I know how it looks Earl, but it just happened. I had no idea Cade was coming home when I decided I couldn't marry you. I'll admit him being here has made it more than clear why it's a good thing we didn't get married, but it just happened."

Earl rolled his eyes, a look of disgust passing over his features. I got pissed because I knew what it had been like when we were together.

"Fine. You get to be pissed, but while you're busy with that, think about how you reacted when I told you I was leaving," I snapped back.

The afternoon I'd been standing in the makeshift dressing room at the church, my thoughts had been spinning so fast on their own little hamster wheel, I'd almost gone through with getting married. But I couldn't. I'd dashed to his dressing room, not really sure I was going to go through with actually breaking up with him. Then, I had. He hadn't even looked particularly upset, more annoyed than anything. He could've fought for me right then, but he didn't even try. Knowing that after the fact, he'd casually announced the wedding was canceled and then gone fishing just summed it all up perfectly. He didn't even let it ruffle the waters of his life.

I hoped for his sake, I truly did, that someday he'd see why I did what I did. Not because I needed him to forgive me because I could live with him blaming me for all of it. Rather, I hoped he'd see what he could have when it happened for him.

His eyes flicked from the chalkboard to me, slightly

wide. Good, maybe he'd start thinking a bit. After a moment, he shook his head. "Whatever, Amelia. If that makes you feel better about your choices, fine. You might want to watch your back though. Shannon's back in town, and I'm pretty sure you can guess why."

A sliver of worry ran through me. I ignored it. I sure as hell didn't need Earl watering those seeds of doubt inside of me. He'd done that well enough by barely bothering to notice me even when we were supposed to be in love.

At that, he muttered something and spun away. "Take care," he said quickly over his shoulder before shouldering his way back outside.

The doorbell jingled cheerily as the door closed behind him. I sighed and turned back to find the person in front of me stepping away. Janet stood behind the counter with a wide smile. "Hey hon, so good to see you. What can I get for you?"

I eyed the chalkboard and then looked at Janet. "Strong coffee and one of your ham and cheese thingies."

Janet chuckled. "Good thing I know what you mean."

She tapped the keyboard and gave me the total before spinning away to pour my coffee. "Give me a few on the ham and cheese to heat it up. By the way, don't listen to Earl," she said, her voice low.

I had wrapped my hands around the paper cup of coffee, savoring the warmth. "Did you just hear our entire conversation?"

Janet shrugged with a sly gleam in her eyes. "I was trying to eavesdrop, hon. I have no shame about that. I don't care about you dumping him because that was the best choice for both of you. He's a nice guy, but he's got just a tad too much ego. Anyway, only thing I care about is that bullshit about Shannon. Don't you even worry about it," she said, her words becoming fierce with her last sentence.

I rolled my eyes and shrugged. "I knew Shannon was back because Lucy heard about it and told me. I'm not worried, except for the fact she'll be stirring up some shit. Does she even know Cade and I are back together?"

Janet returned the eye roll. "She does as of this morning. I made sure to tell her when she showed up here with her sister. Trust me, she looked surprised. Can't say I blame her. If she had her ear to the ground, the news you'd bolted on Earl would've traveled to her slowly since she's been in Anchorage. I don't give a damn, but she pissed me off before, and I told her that today. I swear, her sister annoys the hell out of me. Gayle isn't a bitch, but she stands by and watches her little sister be one. Least she could do is call her out on her shit. Since she won't, I will."

I stared at Janet and almost burst out laughing. Everything with Cade was so fragile and new, it worried me knowing Shannon had blown into town again. I didn't trust her. At all. But I didn't mind having friends like Janet get my back. As far as I was concerned, Shannon getting shamed for what she'd done wouldn't be a bad thing. What I couldn't figure out was why Shannon was so stuck on Cade.

I took a gulp of my coffee and bit back my bitter laugh. "Thanks Janet. I know you've got my back. I'm just hoping she gets the message loud and clear. I'm not up for dealing with her. I'm really not."

Janet waved her hand dismissively and spun around when the bell dinged at the server counter. She snagged my ham and cheese roll and handed it over on a plate. "You have nothing to worry about. But people gossip, and they like drama. You and Cade have given them plenty to talk about, but Shannon showing up like this stirs up ugly shit. Ignore it. Don't believe anything you hear. Cade loves you. He always did. Time and distance made you both stupid."

I sensed someone approaching from behind, so I stepped to the side. "I'll do my best. Thanks for being you."

Janet waved me off. "Go sit down and dry off."

Chapter Twenty-Six
CADE

I leaned against the inside of the garage bay door at the front of the fire station and dragged my sleeve across my face. I'd spent the last few hours tuning up my old favorite motorcycle.

"See you got your old bike ready to roll again."

I glanced up to find Beck entering the garage from a side door. "Yup. My dad pulled it out of the back of my parents' garage over the weekend and dropped it off here for me to tune up."

Beck came to lean beside me, casting an approving gaze over the bike. I loved this motorcycle. It was an old Indian and couldn't be purchased new anymore. Just finding one used cost an arm and a leg and then some. When I'd moved to California, I left this bike behind, figuring I wouldn't have time to ride. I'd found time, but I hadn't wanted to bring this baby there. At the time, I'd hated the fact I thought of Amelia whenever I thought of this bike, but that's how it was. I'd logged more miles on it with her than without. Now I could enjoy it and enjoy thinking about her. Win, win.

Beck rolled his head to the side with a slow grin. "Damn

fine bike. Didn't know you'd left this thing in storage up here the whole time. I'd have been happy to ride her for you."

I chuckled and shook my head. "Dude, you can use my other bike, but not this one."

Beck shrugged. "Oh well. You'd best not leave it here. Too tempting for someone else to ride."

"No worries. I planned to take it out to Amelia's place tonight. Figured today was a good day to tune it up, seeing as the weather sucks. Rain's finally stopped though, so I can enjoy the ride without rain."

Beck nodded and slipped his hands in his pockets. "I popped in to let you know Shannon's out front asking to see you. This is when it's nice Maisie's so cranky. I happened to be passing by, and she told Shannon you hadn't mentioned anyone stopping in for a meeting with that *stone cold don't give a damn* look she throws around," Beck said with a low laugh.

"What the fuck is Shannon doing here?" I asked, running a hand through my hair and kicking my heel against the garage door behind me. The sound of my boot hitting the heavy-duty steel door sent an echo through the cavernous garage. Not only did I not want to deal with Shannon, but now I had to worry about how Amelia might react.

Beck shrugged. "Hell if I know. She sat herself down and said she'd wait. Want me to chase her off?"

I shook my head. "Nah. I'll deal with it. Dude, I haven't seen Shannon since she pulled that shit trying to hook up with me. Fuck, I'd better tell Amelia."

I slipped my phone out of my pocket and punched in a text.

No idea what's up. Shannon's here. Figured you might want to know.

I looked to Beck and rolled my eyes. "Any suggestions on how to get her to get a fucking clue?"

Beck shrugged. "Dude, you are way more experienced with relationships than me."

I threw a faux glare Beck's way. "Man, the only relationship I've ever had was and is with Amelia. I'd say you're way more experienced at chasing off women than me."

Beck started laughing, and my phone beeped.

I glanced down to see Amelia's response.

Ugh. Forgot to tell you last night. Lucy heard she's back.

I tapped out a swift reply.

Uh, coulda told me. Heads up would've been nice.

Uh, we were busy. With much better things.

I grinned and could practically see her grin. So true. We'd been quite busy with each other.

Right. Things we'll be busy with later. Meantime, she showed up here at the station. Beck's not so helpful telling me how to chase her off.

Tell her to go to hell.

I glanced up at Beck. "Amelia says to tell her to go to hell."

Beck grinned. "Sounds like a plan."

I looked back at my phone screen.

On it. Where are you?

Firehouse Café. What time will you be home?

Damn. A simple question, and my heart kicked so hard, my chest ached. I loved this woman so damn much. Home was Amelia, and she wanted to know when I'd be there.

Just have to tell Shannon to go to hell. Then I'm taking my bike home. Ride tonight?

YES! □

Grinning, I slipped my phone back in my pocket to find Beck's perceptive gaze on me.

"What?" I asked.

"Dude, you are whipped. Damn good thing you came home," Beck said.

Just a few shorts months ago, I'd have glared at anyone who even proposed the idea I might be whipped by any woman. Hell, I'd been so bitter, I didn't even give myself many opportunities for even casual sex. Here and there, I'd caved because I was a man and I had needs. But it had always come up short because no one, absolutely no one, could live up to what I had with Amelia. I was so fucking relieved we were back together.

I met Beck's amused gaze with a shrug. "Sure am." I pushed away from the door. "I'm gonna go tell Shannon to go to hell and then head home."

Beck walked alongside me. "You sound downright cheerful about it."

I paused at the door into the front area and clapped Beck on the shoulder. "You just haven't met the right woman. You will and then you'll get it."

At that, I pushed through the door, Beck muttering behind me. "Whatever dude."

I strode past Maisie's desk. She managed not to glare at me, which I considered progress on her part. Shannon sat in one of the chairs in the waiting area. She stood quickly when she saw me. "Cade! I can't believe you're home."

Shannon started to walk toward me, stopping when I held a hand up. I knew Shannon was used to catching attention from men. Objectively speaking, she was beautiful with her long dark hair, bright blue eyes, and curvy figure. She didn't do a thing for me, but I wasn't blind. I'd never mentioned it to Amelia way back when, but I'd never quite understood her friendship with Shannon. Shannon was too competitive, too pushy.

Shannon's over-the-top smile faded when I held my hand up like a damn stop sign. She stood where she was and clasped her hands together. I could practically see the gears shifting in her brain.

"Hey Shannon. Just came out here to tell you to go to hell."

I spun on my heel, ignoring her gasp as I strode back to the door.

Footsteps sounded rapidly behind me, and she grabbed my arm. "Cade! I can't believe…"

I spun back. Now I was pissed. "Don't fucking touch me.

There was *never* anything with us and never will be. I'm home, and I'm back with Amelia. You won't be able to pull a stunt like the one you did before with your bullshit."

I shook her hand off of my arm and stepped to the door. Shannon was silent with two bright spots of color high on her cheeks. Resignation was evident on her face. I glanced to Maisie. "Maisie, there will never be a circumstance when Shannon would have my permission to be here unless it's an actual emergency. Please don't allow her in the back under any circumstance."

Maisie held my gaze, her wide brown eyes firm. She nodded emphatically. "Of course. I already told her today she couldn't go back, but now I know for sure."

Shannon's eyes darkened. "Fuck you, Cade. You can't..."

"Don't even try it. I don't know what your deal is, and frankly, I don't give a shit. If you upset Amelia in any way, you'll regret it."

I walked past her and opened the entry door, gesturing for her to leave. She flounced past me, but didn't say another word. I let the door fall closed and turned back. Maisie was studiously looking at something on her computer screen.

I walked to the reception desk and glanced over the counter at her. "Thanks Maisie."

She looked up, and for the first time, I saw a hint, just the barest glimmer, of uncertainty under her prickly bravado. "You're welcome. You're really good about letting me know your schedule, so when she showed up I figured you didn't have an appointment with her." She paused and chewed on the inside of her cheek, her gaze considering. "I really want to do a good job. I'm sorry you guys had to tell me to be nicer," she blurted out.

"Maisie, you already do a good job. You're responsible, on time and you haven't missed a single day of work. We're all appreciative that you're trying to be a little friendlier. Trust me, we all have our days." I paused and threw her a grin. "If you want to be cranky with Shannon, have at it."

"I won't be too bitchy, but you tell me if she bothers Amelia, and I'll kick her ass. I can actually fight," Maisie said with a sly grin.

I laughed so hard, I got tears in my eyes. When I caught my breath, Beck was walking through the door from the garage, glancing between us as if we were aliens.

"What the hell? You smile?" Beck asked, his startled gaze swinging to Maisie.

Maisie immediately flushed and looked back down at her computer. I looked to Beck. "Maisie offered to kick Shannon's ass."

It was Beck's turn to laugh, and I was relieved to see Maisie's small smile reappear.

Chapter Twenty-Seven
AMELIA

I rested my cheek against Cade's back as we rode along a winding road that headed toward the ocean. Willow Brook wasn't right on the coast, but it was roughly a half hour away. I'd been anxious for Cade to get home once he'd told me he had his bike. We'd taken many trips—short and long—on this very motorcycle before. I hadn't even known he still owned it, but apparently this bike, his favorite, had been stored in the back of his parents' garage all this time.

He'd purchased a new helmet for me on his way home, announcing he couldn't find the old one I'd used years ago. With my arms looped about his waist, I lifted my head and savored the cool summer air. This road avoided Anchorage entirely and skipped down to the shoreline along Cook Inlet, the wide inlet from the Gulf of Alaska in the Pacific Ocean that stretched inland to Anchorage. We were headed towards a viewing point along Turnagain Arm, the aptly named branch off the inlet the road followed, turning again and again and again along the water's edge.

As we traveled south from Willow Brook, the woodsy mountain air started to mingle with the crisp, salty ocean breezes. I felt as if I were sipping the scents of life when I rode on the back of Cade's motorcycle. The trees started to thin and the view opened up as we reached Turnagain Arm, which offered a view nothing short of spectacular with the feet of the mountains kissing the water's edge. The engine rumbled as Cade downshifted and eased onto a narrow side road almost hidden by the trees. Turnagain Arm itself was a busy place for traffic all summer long, seeing as it was the only way for travelers to get from Anchorage onto the Alaskan playground that was the Kenai Peninsula. The Kenai Peninsula was home to rivers, the ocean, sparkling bays and several communities that catered to tourists, chief among them Diamond Creek and Homer.

Cade skipped off that busy road onto a narrow dirt road that led us to a secluded viewing area, known only to locals and definitely not accessible by campers. It was also completely unmarked, so only the rare, adventurous tourist might stumble upon it. Through a cluster of birch, the road opened up to a grassy bluff. He rolled to a stop and glanced over his shoulder, flashing one of his devastating grins.

Being with him was an odd combination of the familiar and the new. Perhaps it was that the familiar felt fresh and sharp. No matter what, his grin had the effect it always had. Liquid need slid through my veins and my belly fluttered. He kicked the stand down and turned the engine off. In a flash, he spun around on the motorcycle seat so he was facing me.

He reached over and unbuckled my helmet, carefully removing it and hooking it on one of the handlebars. I started to return the favor, but he beat me to it.

We sat in silence for a moment. My ears readjusted to the absence of the humming engine, the sound of birds chattering in the trees and the water rolling softly against the shore percolating around us.

Cade looked away, his eyes scanning the span of water. Turnagain Arm was a narrow offshoot from Cook Inlet. The mountains on the other side were so close, it felt as if you could reach over and touch them. Gulls called and swooped, a patch of bright pink flowers stood out at the edge of the sand where the grass ended, and the briny scent of the ocean gusted on the breeze.

"I forgot how much I loved it here," Cade said gruffly, his gaze coming back to land on me.

"I haven't been here since the last time I came with you."

My words came out husky, and emotion pressed hot tears in my eyes and tightened like a band around my heart. The intensity of the feeling crashed over me suddenly. I'd tried so hard—so, so hard—not to dwell on him when he was gone. I'd clung to my anger like the lifeboat it had been. Without it, I'd likely have fallen to pieces inside. Sadly, my resolute determination to keep thoughts of him at bay—which if I were being honest with myself had completely failed—led to me shutting out any conversation about him and the glaring reality I'd never allowed myself to find out the truth of what had happened. I'd also avoided certain places—places that were tied too tightly to my memories of him. This was one of them. This officially nameless spot that we'd dubbed *Again Beach* because we used to go here again and again.

Here we were—again—my first visit after seven years away. It was fitting, of course, that I was with Cade. He watched me quietly, his eyes darkening with concern.

"You really haven't been here since then?"

His question felt quiet and heavy with the portent of what my words meant.

I swallowed and bit my lip, shaking my head quickly before snapping my eyes away. It was almost too much, too intense, to look at him. When I felt emotional like this, not a common thing for me, I felt vulnerable and exposed. Even worse, I'd fought so hard to build up my emotional armor after the way things ended with him. I could see where my own stubbornness had become my worst enemy, but newly developed awareness didn't erase time or the defenses I'd developed to learn how to cope.

His thumb brushed across my bottom lip, and I flicked my gaze back to him.

"Hey, you okay?" he asked.

I nodded, a tad too rapidly. I forced myself to take a slow breath, my shoulders sagging when I let it out.

"Yes and no," I finally said. "Yes, because it's so good to have you home and to have you here. No, because I feel like an idiot for getting so pissed off before and not giving us some time to talk."

His eyes were considering. After a beat, he lifted a shoulder in a shrug. "It sucks, but we were both pretty stubborn. I could've tried a little harder to push it. It sure as hell didn't help that I was so far away for so long. We can't change the past." He paused, his gaze turning inward as if considering what he meant to say. "I took your advice."

My confusion must have shown on my face because he continued quickly. "I told Shannon to go to hell."

I burst out laughing. "Oh my God! Really? How'd she take it?"

"I don't think she was too happy, but I didn't give her much chance to talk. There's nothing to talk about. Honestly..." He paused, his hand dropping to grip mine. "I don't know what the fuck her deal is. She was never my favorite friend of yours back in the day, but did I miss something? There was never anything there with us that I noticed. Next thing I know she's hopping in bed and you're storming out. I haven't talked to her since I told her to fuck off before." The furrow in his brow cleared, and he grinned. "Maisie's default bitch mode was helpful. She wouldn't let Shannon out back at the station—thank fucking God—and then offered to kick her ass if I needed her to. Oh, and she told me she knows how to fight."

I laughed so hard, tears rolled down my cheeks. When I caught my breath, I looked back at Cade. "Normally, I'd wonder if you were exaggerating, but with Maisie, I don't doubt it for a second." I scrubbed the end of my sleeve on my cheeks and took a deep breath, savoring the crisp ocean air. "I don't know what Shannon's deal is. Honestly, I put up a firewall around conversations about you after what happened. Shannon and I never talked again. I'll have to ask Lucy what she knows. You'd think I'd be wondering, but having you back is taking up all my head space, so…" I ended with a shrug, flushing at his direct gaze.

He eased his grip on my hand and rested both of his on my hips. "So we're good? You're not freaked out about her pulling this bullshit today?"

I wanted to shrug it off. If none of this involved my heart, I'd have been able to say it was fine. As it was, my heart was so tangled up with Cade, it was impossible to shrug anything off. I could tell myself intellectually that I should feel okay, and I did. Mostly.

I felt as if he was looking inside my head, or perhaps my heart. His eyes scanning my face, his shoulders rose and fell with a breath. "I fucking hate that you would even worry all because she pulled that stunt. You know I had nothing to do with her, right? Nothing," he said vehemently.

I chewed on the inside of my cheek, feeling bad that I still had these weird insecurities. It wasn't just what Cade told me, but now that I'd stopped shutting out any and all talk related to him, it was pretty clear there'd never been anything to him and Shannon. Yet, old habits died hard. The perceived betrayal had scored me so deeply, the pain was still there. I looked back at him and saw nothing but fierce tenderness in his gaze, so I shoved those stupid, clingy insecurities away. "I know, I know. Just like you couldn't stand to see me anywhere near Earl even though you knew there was nothing going on, it's hard to know Shannon's around because I don't know what she might do. It's not really a rational thing."

He nodded slowly, his mouth curling at one corner in a wry smile. "No, 'spose not."

I took another breath and gave myself a mental shake.

"No need to keep talking about it. Seeing as I'm not rational about it, that doesn't really help," I said with a soft laugh.

"You sure? Because I'll talk all day and all night if it would help."

I knew by the look in his eyes, he would. Knowing Cade, usually armored with his *don't give a damn* attitude, I loved that I got to see the other side of him. He wasn't much of a talker. He was all action.

"I'm sure." I lifted a hand and traced along his jawline.

His eyes darkened, and he slid his hands up my waist, brushing past the sides of my breasts. My breath hitched and heat pooled low in my belly.

"Good because I don't really want to talk about her anymore," he said, his gravelly voice sending hot shivers over my skin.

With my pulse skittering wildly, I let my gaze coast over him. Sweet hell. It was too much. Beyond the blatant, fiery desire I felt for him, he was about as alpha masculine as a man could get and not be obnoxious about it. He sat there, inches away from me, in his faded black jeans that fit his muscled legs like a glove, his black t-shirt paired with his black leather jacket. With his rumpled brown curls and hooded green gaze on me, I figured I might as well just melt right here. I could feel the slick heat between my thighs and my heart thudding against my ribs.

After a beat, he stroked his palm around my back, tangling his hand in my hair and fitting his mouth over mine. In a flash, the heated, still moment went up in a burst of flames. Kissing him was like tumbling into madness. His kisses were rough and wet, soft and gentle, and everything all at once—sweeping his tongue in for deep strokes, pulling back and catching my bottom lip in his teeth, tracing my mouth with his tongue. All the while, his hands were busy toying with my nipples, adjusting the angle of our kiss to trail a blaze of wet fire down my neck and into the V of my t-shirt. He leaned back long enough to shove my shirt down and flick the clasp on my bra. My breasts bounced free, and I groaned when he leaned forward and drew a nipple into his mouth. The suction alone nearly made me climax.

With him, I was always teetering on the edge, chasing the sharp bite of pleasure. When he turned his attention to my other breast, my nipple a tight bead of expectation, I cried out sharply and buried my hands in his hair, needing something to hold onto. The contrasting cool air hitting my damp skin only notched the heat inside higher.

I hadn't realized I'd all but straddled his lap on the motorcycle until the sound of a vehicle approaching nudged me out of my wild daze. Cade heard the sound at the same time I did and lifted his head, quickly tugging my shirt up. I glanced down and bit back a laugh. My damp nipples were easily visible through my t-shirt, while my bra was askew. He eased back from me in the nick of time, creating barely enough space between us to pass as decent, when a battered truck rolled through the trees into the clearing by the water.

Cade caught my eyes, a sly gleam in his. "Walk?"

I shook my head.

"No walk? But this is the first time we've been back here."

The occupants of the truck climbed out, two men wearing fishing waders. They waved as they walked by after gathering fishing gear from the back of the truck. They disappeared out of sight momentarily when they walked down the steep path along the small bluff to the water. Within moments, they were casting their lines.

Alone again, I glanced back to Cade, my body humming from his closeness. "No walk," I said, leaning forward until my lips were brushing against his with my words.

The heat of his hands sliding up my thighs nearly made me tackle him right there. "Rain check on the walk only if you promise we'll come back soon," he murmured against my lips.

It took all of my willpower to contain myself, but I really wasn't up for giving the two fishermen a show.

"Promise," I whispered.

Cade pushed back on the seat and swung his leg over, quickly handing over my helmet, while he put his own on. In seconds, the engine of his bike rumbled to life, that low, throaty growl I associated solely with him even when I heard it from a distance and knew he was nowhere near.

Chapter Twenty-Eight
CADE

I leaned my head against the headboard and glanced over to the bathroom. Amelia stood in the doorway brushing her teeth.

"When'd you say you had to go to Fairbanks?" she asked, her question surprisingly clear amidst the tooth brushing.

Before I answered, she spun around and ran the faucet while she rinsed. I figured there wasn't much better than Amelia walking around bare-ass naked while she got ready for bed. I was let down when she snagged one of my t-shirts and tossed it over her head before crawling in bed beside me.

"You didn't answer me," she said as she adjusted the blankets and grabbed the remote.

"Day after tomorrow," I said as she settled against my side, hooking her foot over my calf and idly tapping the remote against my chest.

We'd made it home after our ride to Turnagain Arm to stumble inside and tear each other's clothes off. After a quick meal of leftover pizza, we'd showered. I closed my eyes, savoring the feel of her against me.

"How long?" came her next question.

"Three days," I replied, opening my eyes and glancing down at her.

"I suppose it's not helpful for me to complain, huh?" she asked, her mouth curling in a rueful grin.

I chuckled. "You can complain. It won't change my job. Once I get through these state mandated certifications, I'll only be taking off when I have to respond to a fire."

She sighed and rolled her head to look toward the television. In the few weeks I'd been staying with her, we'd fallen into our old habit of watching a few shows at night. As good as things felt, I sensed a thread of uncertainty emanating from her about me traveling. I understood it because I felt it too. Everything was so fresh, still on shaky ground as if a jolt at the wrong time could rattle us far more than it should.

I sifted my fingers through her hair.

"I know," she said softly.

After a few minutes, her breathing evened out. I slowly pulled the remote out of her hand and set it on the nightstand before reaching to flick the lamp off. I eased down into the pillows. She never woke, her body adjusting to my motion and sinking against me.

I looked down at the landscape below. I'd finished my third day of training in Fairbanks, three days of boring, administrative crap. I thrived in my job, loved just about all aspects of it. I didn't mean that I loved putting myself or my crew in danger, but I knew what it meant, so I did it. The one and only thing I didn't like about my job was the admin side of things. I missed Amelia like crazy and wanted to get back to Willow Brook yesterday.

We'd been about to hop on a return plane when I got the call my crew was called out for a rotation on a fire in the

Alaskan Interior. Alaska had so many vast swaths of forest, a number of fires were simply managed as there was nothing to worry about. This fire was moving fast and headed straight toward a cluster of small communities in the Interior.

The mountains on the outskirts of Fairbanks receded in the distance as the land gradually shifted into vistas of forest interspersed with fields. I glanced to the pilot.

"Any idea how long before we reach the fire?" I asked.

The pilot, a jovial man named Fred Banks, kept his eyes trained ahead. "I'd say we've got another half hour. I'll set us down in a lake nearby. When I was out here the other day, they had their main station set up there. You spent much time in Alaska?"

"Oh yeah. Born here. Grew up in Willow Brook."

Fred glanced my way, flashing a grin, his blue eyes twinkling in his weathered face. "I figured you for a transplant when Beck mentioned you'd done your training in California. My mistake."

I shrugged. "Easy mistake to make. I stayed there for seven years, so it's been a bit. I've never flown out where we're headed though. Taken plenty of trips hiking and fishing all over, but not there."

"It's wild country out here. With the beetle kill, as I'm sure you know, these fires have been worse every year. They've had the local crews trying to beat it back, but it's too big now."

I would typically be flying out here with my crew from Willow Brook and more likely in a helicopter rather than a plane. Yet, every available helicopter service in Fairbanks was booked, so Maisie had tracked down Fred and scheduled for me to fly out to rendezvous with the crew on site.

I glanced out the small plane's window and watched the rolling hills dotted with lakes here and there pass beneath them. I'd called Amelia before heading out and flat hated that I couldn't see her before this job. I figured I might eventually get accustomed to jaunting off and leaving her behind, but I damn sure didn't like it right about now.

Just thinking about her sent my heart to thudding inside my chest. Of all the things I'd never thought I'd have to worry about again, it was the ache of missing someone when I headed out to the field to face fires. I forced my mind back to the moment because I didn't really like thinking about Amelia, not like this.

Fred's estimate was dead on. He eased the floatplane into a near-perfect landing on what would've been a picturesque lake under normal circumstances. Instead, the trees and ground in the surrounding area where charred. The fire had passed through this area roughly a week prior. The fire had spread rapidly and expanded to over one thousand acres inside of a week. I had this fire on my radar and been expecting my crew to get called out if it continued to grow.

Once the plane landed, Fred taxied over to a floating dock at the edge of the lake. He helped me unload and followed me over to a cluster of tents. Within minutes, I was in the midst of a discussion with the foreman for the local crew from Fairbanks. I radioed my crew who were scheduled to land in the area within the hour.

Time raced as crews rotated in and out, helicopters landed to refill with water from the lake to carry out over the fire, and I geared up to head out to a corner section of the fire with my crew.

Late that night with the sky wispy light and smoke drifting through the air, I rested against a boulder and glanced to Levi Phillips, holding out a protein bar for him. "Another?" I asked.

Levi flashed a tired grin and snagged it from me. "Amazing how good these things are when you're starving."

I nodded and rubbed the corner of my sleeve on my face. We'd been working our asses off all afternoon to create a firebreak over in this corner. A wide, shallow river ran through this area. We were using the river's natural barrier and adding to it by clearing all flammable fuel from the grasses and forest out of the fire's way. Two other crews were working on containment in other sections of the massive fire. I'd been so busy, my mind had conveniently stopped spinning its wheels over missing Amelia. Now that we were calling it for the night, she was back in my thoughts.

"Hard to believe it's after midnight," Levi commented.

I looked up to the sky. In this part of Alaska, there were a few days of barely a sunset. We were past that time of summer, but I'd guess the sun might only set for a few hours tonight. Stars glittered against the dusky sky with the moon visible in the distance through the haze of smoke filling the horizon as far as the eye could see.

"Yeah. Even though I'm used to the long days and short nights, this is more light than we get in Willow Brook."

Levi snorted. "Definitely more light than what I'm used to from Juneau, seeing as that's further south."

I eyed the other guys. We were sprawled about the area by the river, a few already crashed out in their sleeping bags. I'd had enough time in Willow Brook to get to know my crew. They were solid guys and worked well together. Levi was one of the squad leaders, steady, reliable and completely unflappable. The other guys looked up to him and listened to him, so it was a great fit.

I was weary and figured I'd probably best try to catch a few winks of sleep. "You up for watch for a little bit?" I asked Levi.

Levi nodded as he took a long drag of water from a bottle. "Sure thing," he said when he set the bottle down. "Thad and I are the night owls. We'll handle this first shift."

I nodded and rolled to standing, striding away and sliding into my sleeping bag. I stared up at the sky for a few minutes, recalling the last time I'd slept outside under the stars in Alaska had been with Amelia.

Chapter Twenty-Nine
AMELIA

I slapped my leather work gloves against my jeans, knocking the dirt loose, and glanced to Lucy who stood beside me, hands on hips as we surveyed our work.

"Are you sure that weird corner window they want isn't going to be a nightmare?" Lucy asked, turning to face me. She had dirt streaked on one cheek, her blonde hair was tumbling loose from its ponytail, and she looked as weary as I felt.

We'd pushed hard today and finished the framing for the home on this project. With Cade's absence an ever-present ache in my heart, so strong it was visceral, I'd thrown myself into work. I looked up to the corner Lucy was referencing. The owners wanted a corner window that was sort of a bay window times two. It wasn't common and involved some extra angles, but I wasn't concerned.

"Nah. We already did the hard part today," I replied with a shrug.

Lucy rolled her eyes. "Yeah, and it was a pain in the ass."

"Right, so we're done now."

Lucy glanced to her watch and back to me. "Damn. It's

almost nine o'clock. You're a workaholic with Cade gone. It's a good thing I have no social life."

I laughed and turned to walk toward our work truck. "You have a social life. You just act like you don't."

Lucy walked alongside me. "Not really. My social life consists of hanging out with you and maybe a few others. Hanging out with you has taken a serious hit since your lover boy moved back. I never thought I'd say Earl was great, but you and him didn't do much together. You and Cade are glued to each other," Lucy grumbled good-naturedly.

I tossed my gloves in the back of the truck and took the toolbox Lucy handed me from where it had been sitting on the ground. I leaned my hips against the truck and eyed Lucy. "I'm sorry. I didn't mean to seem like I was blowing you off."

Lucy's eyes softened. "Hey girl, just teasing. I'm happy for you. Cade obviously adores you. It's just an adjustment for me. Even though you weren't single, you kinda were with Earl. Now I have to get used to my bestie actually having a life."

I felt my cheeks heat and was relieved for the wispy light of the late evening. "I guess it's been so good to have Cade home that I kinda shut everything else out. My mom stopped by last night and said something along the same lines. Even when he's back from the fire, let's make sure we have girls' night at least once a week. But before that, let's plan to finish work at a halfway decent hour tomorrow and grab some dinner and drinks at Wildlands."

Lucy flashed a grin and stepped close to throw her arms around me for a quick hug. When she stepped back, her eyes were warm. "I really was just teasing, you know?"

"I know, but still. Even if it's awesome to have Cade back and things seem to be going great with us, I can't let him take over my life." I paused and eyed Lucy. "Plus, are you ever even going to think about dating? Man, woman, fish, bear? Anyone?"

Lucy burst out laughing and swatted me on the arm. "It just never seems worth the trouble. You know the bears, the fish and the women aren't my thing. But then men aren't really either. I think I'm too me."

I snorted. "You're too *you*? What the hell does that mean?"

Lucy crossed her arms and shrugged. I could feel her defensiveness. Lucy might have become my closest friend over the last few years, but Lucy definitely had *stuff* she preferred not to talk about, most particularly relationships. I knew enough about her to piece together that something had gone sideways at some point before she moved to Willow Brook in high school, but Lucy never spoke of it and was an expert at friendly evasion.

Maybe it was because I'd just had my own major jolt of awareness when I almost married a man I didn't love and who didn't love me. Maybe it was because it seemed like now was an okay time to push a little, but I did. I looked over at Lucy when Lucy looked away and pressed her. "Seriously, Lucy. I could care less if you told me you wanted to be single for the rest of your life, or if you said you were an alien who couldn't consider mating with a human, but that's not it. You're so awesome and funny and even though you dress like a man, you are fucking gorgeous and don't even try to argue with me on that. Something happened and you don't have to tell me about it, but maybe think about what it means to let something rule your life like that. I get it because I did. It may not seem like much, but I fell apart after everything blew up with Cade. I let that rule too many choices I made and almost made a huge mistake because of it. I don't know what it is that makes it so you try to act like no one is ever worth it when it comes to romance. Maybe they're not, but let it be because that's what you really want not just because you're scared."

Lucy went still while I spoke, so still I started to worry I'd miscalculated. "Hey, look…"

Lucy shook her head sharply, her blue eyes blazing bright in the dusky light. "It's okay. I'd say something about like this to you if the situation were reversed. I've been beating myself up for not being more pushy with you about Earl. I probably would've if I'd seen you and Cade together the first go-round."

Objectively, I knew Lucy was a petite person, but I tended to forget because Lucy carried herself with such a sense of forcefulness. She came across as strong, confident, and independent, and she was all of those things. But right now, she looked diminished. Her small shoulders rose and fell with a deep breath.

Lucy looked away and then back again. "Someday I might talk about it more, but let's just say high school sucked for me. When we moved here, it was amazing because no one knew me and pretty much left me alone and that was so much better."

I wasn't sure what to say, so I stepped to Lucy and pulled her into a hug, trying to impart the same kind of strength I felt when Lucy hugged me. When I drew back, Lucy's expression had regained some of its zest. She chewed on the inside of her cheek and eyed me. "You driving?"

"Yup." I tugged the keys out of my pocket and hopped in the truck.

In short order, we were in the back parking lot behind the office. Lucy waved as she climbed into her car and drove away. I checked to make sure I'd locked up and headed out in my car, aiming straight for the grocery store. In the short time Cade had been away, I'd slid right back to my old habits of eating mostly takeout and quick dinners. With Cade around, we both liked to cook, but without him here, I wasn't much interested.

Before heading home, I stopped by the grocery store. I was meandering through, laughing at myself as I shopped because I kept wanting to buy items for meals I wanted to make with Cade, yet I didn't even know when he'd be home.

I was dawdling in the produce section when I felt someone stop beside me. I glanced over to see Shannon standing there. A fierce flash of anger jolted me. On its heels was a spinning, falling feeling where everything felt off kilter, and I was hot and cold inside. I hated the fact Shannon had any effect on me, but she did.

Shannon's long dark hair was drawn away from her face with a bright blue headband, which matched her eyes. She rested a hand on her hip and eyed me. "Hello," she finally said.

I stared at her, trying to beat back the sick feeling churning in my stomach and wondering what the hell to say. Shannon had once been my friend, or so I'd believed. We'd both grown up in Willow Brook and been close in middle school and high school. We'd gone to college in different areas, so we'd grown apart, but I had never worried about Shannon trying to make a move on Cade back then. As I stood there, considering what to say, I realized I didn't owe Shannon a damn thing. There was that and the fact I could hardly stand to see her. I didn't like it, but those old seeds of doubt she'd planted inside about me and about Cade were still there. Cade and I were too fresh, too new again for me to feel solid yet. It was also terrifying to think about allowing myself to trust in us again because I had before. Completely. After a moment, I turned and started to walk away.

I stopped abruptly when I felt Shannon's hand curl around my arm. I gave it a rough shake and spun back. "Don't."

Shannon shook her head, her cheeks bright and her eyes angry. "Grow up, Amelia. Are you going to pretend like I don't exist forever?"

My mouth fell open. I snapped it shut. "Shannon, you manufactured the whole fucking thing with Cade before. All of it was you and all of it was a lie. I guess you can feel proud because it worked, but not anymore. Leave me alone, and leave Cade alone."

Shannon shook her head in disgust, something shifting subtly in her eyes. "Tell yourself whatever story you want. Cade's gone again, isn't he?"

I forced my expression to stay calm, but instantly my thoughts were spinning. How did Shannon know anything about where Cade was?

Shannon drummed her fingertips on the cart handle, a sneer curling her lips. "I'm sure you're wondering how I might know anything about Cade's schedule. Why don't you keep on wondering?"

I didn't dare let Shannon dictate this encounter. Fury knotting in my chest, I forced myself to stay calm. Without a word, I turned and walked away. I wanted to run, but I didn't. I measured my steps on the way to the checkout register.

I managed to get through that without losing my shit and walked quickly out to the parking lot. I set the groceries on the passenger seat and climbed into the car. My phone chirped, and I slipped it out of my pocket to see Cade's name flash on the screen. Tapping the banner, his text opened up.

Hey babe, got some cell reception when we flew over just now. Won't be back for three more days at least. Miss you.

That did it. I should've been happy he texted. Instead, all the ugliness and doubt I thought I'd cast aside were spinning in a tight circle in my mind. Seeing Shannon made me feel physically ill. Everything was all tangled up, and I just wanted to go home and forget about it all. My heart was pounding in a frantic, shallow beat and my breath was short. I couldn't love someone the way I loved Cade and fall apart like this. I kept trying to tell myself Shannon was just playing games.

I was so fraught, I never replied to Cade's text.

Chapter Thirty
CADE

The heat of the fire gusted across us with the wind. We were working rapidly to finish clearing the firebreak we'd created by the river. I'd pushed past the brink of exhaustion and kept at it, brutally cutting down small trees and brush. I knew the rest of the crew was as tired as I was. We'd been lucky for two days and nights with the fire moving in the opposite direction, but our luck had changed along with the wind. I hadn't slept for over twenty-four hours at this point. Once the wind shifted late the evening before last, we'd been hard at work with breaks few and far between.

I was working so fast, I didn't even notice I was about to collide with the edge of a bluff until I did. I paused and glanced up at the rocky face. We'd reached the end of the work we could do here and needed to fall back and hope for the best. I glanced back in the direction I'd been moving to see the flames flickering against the hazy sky in the distance. The sound of helicopter blades rumbled in the distance as one flew above, dropping fire retardant atop the flames.

As the remainder of the crew caught up with me, we checked in after I radioed the main base. "We'll sit tight here until a helicopter can come out for pick up. Our break is holding where we started it miles away, so the plan is to rotate us out tonight if they can. We'll spend the night at the main camp and fly home day after tomorrow," I said, scanning the crew. Everyone's faces were streaked with soot, dust and sweat.

Levi stood in the middle, one hand resting on his hip as he let his gear bag fall off his shoulders. "We clear to rest for a bit while we wait?" he asked.

"Not much else to do," I replied. "Fire's still moving, but the wind seems to be slowing down and it's not jumping the river, so here's hoping the break holds." I paused and looked past the river at the fire flickering in the distance. I looked back at the crew. "We kicked ass on this section. Sounds like the Fairbanks crew has done a bang up job of containing the corner closest to Chena. If the breaks hold, we might be able to tamp this fire down enough."

I got some weary grins, although I knew damn well they were just as tired as I was, and I was on my last legs. Within a few minutes, we were scattered about the ground by the river, munching on protein bars and guzzling water. There wasn't much conversation. I leaned against a boulder by the river, Amelia immediately strolling into my thoughts. I hadn't thought about her much because I'd been focused entirely on the work of dealing with the fire, but the niggling worry I'd had meandered right back into my mind. She'd never replied to my text. I didn't have reception worth a damn out here, but I would once I got up in the air. I'd have to wait until then to find out if she ever had.

I must've dozed off because I woke abruptly at the deafening sound of a helicopter coming down to land. I sat up quickly to see the helicopter settling to the ground a short distance away. The pilot climbed out and waved. I wasn't the only one who'd fallen asleep. I circled the group, nudging a few guys with my boot, until they were all on their feet and carrying their heavy gear to the helicopter. The problem with rest when we were deep in the backcountry was that once you were out, it was hard to get back up to speed simply for the sheer exhaustion of the work we'd been doing.

The pilot flashed a grin at the sight of us and clapped me on the shoulder. "You guys are overdue to be pulled out. Damn hard few days with the wind."

I nodded wearily. "We'd keep going, but it looks like we can pull back for now. How's it looking overall?"

"Still burning hot in some areas, but the containment is working. Cut it down by a few thousand acres," the pilot replied.

The pilot moved swiftly, tossing gear into the hold at the bottom of the helicopter. Inside of a few minutes, he'd herded us into the helicopter and readied for takeoff.

Conversation was out once the motor was whirring and the blades whacking through the air. Once we were airborne, I leaned my head back and closed my eyes with a sigh. I might be in peak physical condition because the job demanded it, but that didn't mean I didn't get sore and weary after two days and nights of working almost straight through.

Roughly an hour later, I heard the pilot speaking into his radio and lifted my head to see the lake where the main camp was set up. I fumbled in my backpack and found my phone. Once it powered up, it took a minute before it picked up reception. Another few seconds and a text banner flashed with Amelia's name on it. Relief rolled through me. I clicked on the text.

Why does Shannon know your schedule?

That text had been sent a few hours after my last text to her, so I could only guess she'd been stewing over something. But what? What the fuck? There had been *nothing*, more than nothing with Shannon beyond the bullshit she manufactured by trying to crawl into bed with me when she knew Amelia would be walking in. I swore and stared out the window, my gut churning. No matter what I did, I wouldn't be able to get back to Amelia for another day or two at the earliest.

I glanced down at my phone screen to see another text had come from her a few hours after the first.

I'm trying not to freak out, but I can't figure out any reason why Shannon would know anything about where you were. I can't handle this if it turns out there was more to the story than you told me.

I swore and ran a hand roughly through my hair. Fuck, fuck, fuck. I had no idea what Shannon was up to, but I didn't trust her. At all. She was a master manipulator. I hated that I was trapped on this helicopter and then at the mercy of the weather and the schedules of various pilots to get out of the main camp, back to Fairbanks, and then back to Anchorage where I could finally drive home.

I glanced around the helicopter to see all but Levi sound asleep. Levi was seated across from me, his eyes scanning the landscape. I gave myself a shake and looked out my window to see how the landscape looked. Flames flickered in various areas with wide swaths of burned trees and ground stretching as far as I could see. The river we'd been working beside wove like a ribbon through the blackened landscape. As we flew over, there were other helicopters visible in the distance.

I glanced back to my phone and beat back the anger and frustration knotting inside. On the heels of a breath, I tapped my screen to reply. We'd blown apart before because of sheer stubbornness and both of us too hurt to reach past it. I'd be damned if I'd lose Amelia again.

I don't know what Shannon told you or what you heard. There is NOTHING going on with Shannon and there NEVER was. I have no f'in idea what she said to you, but I can guess she said something. Please, please don't listen to her. I should be home by day after tomorrow. If you get worried, remember I love you.

I hit send and held my phone loosely in my hand. I wished I were home because trying to have a conversation over text made me feel so damn helpless. I had so many feelings and I couldn't pour them through a text. I wanted to hold her and impart everything through my hands and body. I took a breath and leaned my head back, whipping it up the moment my phone vibrated in my hand.

Failure to send.

Oh hell. I breathed through the tightness in my chest. This text better fucking send. I opened it up and hit send again.

A few seconds passed.

Failure to send.

Chapter Thirty-One
AMELIA

I kicked the dirt off of my boots before pushing through the swinging door into the Firehouse Café. Lucy was right behind me with the distinctive thump of her boots hitting the edge of the threshold. The rain had thwarted our work schedule for the day, so we'd come here for a late lunch.

Once we ordered and were seated with hot coffees to warm our nearly numb hands, I leaned back in my chair with a sigh. "Damn. Summer's nice, but when it rains, summer disappears."

"Summer in Alaska only counts when the sun's out. Otherwise, it's not summer," Lucy replied firmly before taking a gulp of her coffee.

Lucy's wide blue eyes coasted over me, her gaze assessing. "Okay, what's up?" she asked sharply.

"Huh?" I returned reflexively. I knew Lucy could sense I wasn't doing too great, but I felt ridiculous about the whole thing, so I was hoping to avoid a conversation.

Lucy's wide eyes narrowed and she leaned forward, resting her elbows on the table. "Don't even try it. You've been cranky as hell for the last few days and all quiet. I know you miss Cade, but something else is going on."

I took a sip of my coffee, savoring the warmth of it, along with the warmth of the café. The chill that had settled in my bones from working in the rain started to ease. I took a breath and let it out with a long sigh. "I'm freaking out because I ran into Shannon at the grocery store the other night and somehow she knew Cade was gone and told me I should wonder what that meant. I can't fall apart like I did before. I know I shouldn't trust her, but it's like sand in my shoe. I can't shake the feeling of worrying maybe I missed something. How the hell does she know anything about his schedule?"

Lucy's lips flattened into a tight line. With a sharp shake of her head and a look of disgust, she replied, "Shannon is a bitch. Plain and simple." Lucy paused to take another swallow of her coffee, her gaze softening as she looked across the table. "It's not exactly hard to find out one of the hotshot crews is out of town. I don't know what Shannon's deal is, but I'm guessing she's just pissy because Cade told her to get the hell out of the way twice now. I barely knew her in high school, but she was the kind of girl who was used to having guys fawn over her. My guess is it probably always bothered her a little that Cade never even noticed her. You'd have to be blind not to notice he's seriously hot. Even worse, he's always had that whole 'don't give a damn' vibe," she said with air quotes.

My confusion must've shown on my face because Lucy sighed elaborately before continuing. "You don't notice because he gives a damn about you. That's what I mean. Back in high school when most guys are so horny they can hardly keep it in their pants for any pretty girl, Cade wasn't like that. He was all distant. Then you two were together and no one could shut up about how perfect you were together. I don't know why Shannon pulled her move the first time around, but I'd say it was simple jealousy. She wasn't used to a guy not noticing her and it bothered her. She'd just been dumped, so that made it worse. Problem now is she's got nothing to lose. She knows she won't be able to have Cade, so why not rattle your cage? She probably feels stupid about what she did and came back thinking she'd try again, but come to find out you and Cade are still in love. It's totally romantic—the whole second chance love thing." Lucy feigned a swoony look.

I stared back at Lucy, not even laughing at her being silly, because I couldn't wrap my brain around the idea Shannon would've been jealous. I mean, in hindsight, I guess it should've been obvious. But Shannon was plain gorgeous and had most guys drooling after her back then. I didn't want to be worried. I really didn't. I just hated how it all felt, even if it was Shannon yanking a chain I didn't even know I had.

Janet arrived at our table right then, saving me from trying to formulate a response. She glanced between us. "What's up?"

"Shannon got Amelia all freaked out by acting like it means something she happened to know Cade was out of town. Please help me remind her Shannon is a total bitch and just playing games because she's got nothing better to do," Lucy said flatly.

Janet rested a hand on her hip, her eyes narrowing. "That girl is just trying to rile you up because that's how she is. She was used to all the guys fawning over her and as long as she had one, she didn't care. Act wore thin because it always does for girls like her. You two stayed friends because you'd known her since she was little. She moved away, did the whole college thing and realized being a little fish in a big pond wasn't much fun. As for why she might know Cade was out of town? You're being stupid. It's not hard to figure out when the whole crew is gone."

"I'm not..."

Janet fixed me with a sharp stare, her look silencing me. "You *are* being stupid. I'll cut you a little slack because Cade hasn't been home long and you two are just figuring things out, but for God's sake, don't let something this dumb get in the way."

My shoulders slumped, and I traced a circle around my coffee mug. "Okay, okay. Maybe I'm being ridiculous," I muttered. Intellectually, I believed everything Janet said. It was my stupid heart that needed more reassurance, specifically in-the-flesh Cade reassurance.

Janet squeezed my shoulder just as her name was called. "What'll it be?" she asked quickly.

We ordered sandwiches before Janet hurried off to the kitchen. I leaned back and eyed Lucy with a rueful smile. "I don't know why it's so easy for Shannon to get to me."

Lucy shrugged. "Because you love Cade, and it really hurt when things fell apart before. I also think you deciding to call off everything with Earl plays into it."

"How?" I asked. Sad to say, once I'd talked to Earl after he'd returned to Willow Brook, I had really and truly moved on from even thinking about him. When I did, I felt sadness tinged with regret for the time we'd wasted, but I didn't miss him.

Lucy continued, "Well, you finally came to your senses about what Earl was to you. No matter how you look at it, that was a big deal. I mean, you were within minutes of marrying the guy. To have that happen and then Cade show back up—coincidentally as far as you two are concerned—well, it would stir some shit up. You decided you didn't want to accept something lukewarm and then scorching hot shows up. You got burned once big time with Cade. It wouldn't have hurt so bad if you hadn't loved him like you did and still do. I'm guessing you're gun-shy. Most people would be. You'll have to get through that with time, but whatever you do, stop letting Shannon pull her bullshit."

I considered Lucy's point and knew immediately she was right on target. I hadn't considered how the reasons behind my choice to break things off with Earl played into it, but it made sense. When Cade was physically here, I was so overcome with the intensity of being with him again, it shoved my doubts and fears far to the back of my mind and heart. With him gone, I missed him so acutely, it reminded me of how I felt after it all fell apart before—a hole in my heart where the pang of emptiness echoed. Adding to the depth of missing him was how everything felt so intense and raw now. I'd loved him before, but the way I felt now eclipsed that love completely. My heart felt full to bursting when he was here, but with him gone, I missed him so much it made me half-crazy. I needed to find some steadiness in the midst of the tumult. Only Cade could do this to me—grab me by the heart, body and soul so hard I felt tossed like a kite in the wind by my emotions.

I stared over at Lucy and took a slow breath. "You're right."

Lucy's eyebrows flew up. "I'm right?"

I sighed and took a sip of coffee. "Yes. That's what I said."

Lucy grinned. "Wow, I don't get that very often."

I rolled my eyes. "I tell you you're right when you're right."

Lucy giggled. "Love ya, hon, but you're stubborn. Just yesterday you wouldn't admit it when I was right about what a fucking nightmare that stupid corner window was gonna be."

I threw my head back with a laugh. "Okay, fine. Sometimes I can be stubborn."

Lucy laughed just as our food arrived. Janet was flying by and slipped our plates in front of us, calling over her shoulder as she spun away, "Need anything else, girls?"

We waved her off and dug into our food. I left a while later, the rain still falling heavily. I drove home and walked into my quiet cabin, Cade's absence an echoing ache in my heart. I'd managed to cobble together a little sense, but it didn't change how much I wanted him home.

Chapter Thirty-Two
CADE

I hooked my hand on the edge of the plane's roof and ducked into the plane. I'd been at the main camp with my crew for two days, bad weather fogging us in. The weather was great because the rain was a godsend at tamping down the massive fire. Flights had been limited to only those necessary, so we were antsy to get out now. A small break in the rain opened up just enough clearing for a few flights this morning. Fred, the very pilot who'd flown me out here, happened to be our pilot this afternoon.

Fred caught my eyes and flashed a grin. "Get in fast guys," he called. "Looks like we've got a small window here."

We hustled into the small plane, this one larger than the two-seater that Fred had flown to get me here with enough seating for six people. The rest of the crew had taken off in another plane minutes ago. I leaned back in my seat and watched the ground roll underneath us as Fred lifted off. The plane leveled and bounced slightly on a gust of wind once we were airborne.

I looked below to see the blackened landscape and smoke rising here and there from the sections of the fire still smoldering under the rain. I hoped the rain would keep at it for another few days. It might be enough to help extinguish the fire completely. I heard Fred speaking into his headset, Fred's brow furrowing at whatever he heard. Another gust of wind bumped the small plane. It was like being in a clothes dryer. These little planes, even a larger one such as this, were so lightweight, they bounced about in the gusts of wind.

Fred carried on, his eyes trained on the horizon. As we flew, the fog that had cleared earlier started to thicken again. Within minutes, I knew we were as good as flying blind in this. Amelia came roaring into my thoughts. In the few days at the main camp, I'd been beyond frustrated with the spotty cell reception. Correction—with the zero cell reception. Every so often, I'd get a signal and try to text or call and nothing ever went through. All I'd done was spin in circles worrying about whatever she was worrying about and feeling helpless because I couldn't talk to her.

Right now, I missed her so hard it hurt. I just wanted to make it to Fairbanks. At least there, I could find my way to Willow Brook no matter the weather. The plane rattled against another strong gust of wind.

Fred spoke into his headset again and then glanced to me. "I've got my coordinates to get us there, but that's it. Hoping for the best," he said curtly.

I nodded because there wasn't much else to say. I glanced around the plane behind me. Without a word passing amongst us, it was obvious every single one of my crew knew this was a shitty situation. I faced forward again and took a slow breath. I faced danger so frequently in the backcountry when I was fighting fires. Yet, that was work I knew, so I didn't experience anxiety or fear because I had my skills and knowledge to fall back on to get me through dicey situations. This though sent a curl of dread through me. We were flying blind over mountains and rivers and not much other than wilderness even where the ground was flat. If anything went wrong, there wasn't a damn thing I could do to stop it.

I kept looking out the window, as if there were anything to see other than thick, gray fog and rain. The small plane cabin felt heavy with tension, every single man in here well aware of how dicey the situation was. I glanced to Fred. "Any idea how much longer we have?"

"Just under a half hour, but I'm not rushing," Fred replied, his words terse.

I looked back out the window, yet again realizing how utterly pointless that was. Another gust of wind sent the plane rocking, and there was an abrupt thump to the right side of the plane. The plane spun sideways. Fred swore and tried to right it. Last thing I remembered was a deafening crack.

Sharp pain shot through my shoulder. I slowly opened my eyes, biting back a groan from the pain. After a beat, I recalled where I was. The plane had crashed. I rolled my head to the side and saw Fred trying to ease his leg out from an odd angle. Okay, so Fred was alive. Check one for thank fucking God. I ignored the pain shooting through my shoulder as I turned in my seat. Everyone but Jesse Franklin had their eyes open. I caught Levi's eyes where he sat beside Jesse. "He okay?" I asked.

Levi, looking as half out of it as I felt, stared blankly for a moment and then turned to Jesse, reaching to check his pulse. Blood ran down Jesse's forehead in a trickle. Levi looked back to me. "Pulse is strong."

I scanned my gaze around. Now that we were on the ground, there was something other than fog to see, although the fog was still thick and I could only see maybe a quarter mile in any direction. We'd landed in a tangle of spruce trees. By the grace of God, nature, or blind luck, we were past the burned part of the forest, so we had the benefit of wide spruce boughs to ease our crash. A glance to my right, I saw the plane's wing broken and figured that must've been the cracking sound I'd heard.

I looked to Fred. "You okay?"

Fred glanced up from where he was maneuvering his calf free from a crushed corner of the plane's nose. "Leg hurts like hell, but I'm alive." He muttered a curse when he finally got his leg out. The denim had blood soaking through it. I started to move and swore at another bolt of pain in my shoulder. I finally tried to see what the problem was and discovered the roof above me had crushed against my shoulder. I couldn't see it, but could feel the warmth of blood seeping and surmised the torn aluminum of the plane's shell had cut into my shoulder.

I used my free hand to reach above and push against the crushed roof. The broken section of aluminum gave way, and I eased my shoulder out. After a quick glance to ascertain I wasn't bleeding profusely, I went into action. The rest of the crew was doing the same thing—everyone dealing with their own minor injuries as they gradually got out of the plane. The good part was the engine itself had stayed mostly untouched, so there was no worry about it catching fire. Jesse appeared to be in the worst shape and was still unconscious. Not for the first time, I was beyond relieved to have an entire crew of trained wilderness medics surrounding me. This might be my first plane crash, but I'd faced many mini medical crises when out in the field and had complete faith we could stabilize Jesse until help arrived.

The other major concern was Fred. He'd sustained a nasty, deep gash running from his ankle to his knee. He was mobile, conscious and clearly in severe pain. Levi and Thad focused on stabilizing Jesse, while Jackson helped me get Fred settled in one of the plane's seats and worked to clean up his wound. The rest of the crew hauled gear out of the plane.

Fred was stubborn and insisted on being in charge of communication through the radio despite the fact he was gritting his teeth with every word. The dispatch in Fairbanks confirmed they would send a medical helicopter out once it was clear to fly. That left the weather as the only remaining concern. As good as the rain and cool weather were for the fire, this weather was prime for hypothermia. It was easy to worry about hypothermia in the dead of winter, but statistically speaking, far more people were subject to its risks in weather like this because it wasn't considered as risky.

Once I felt good that Fred's bleeding was under control and Jesse was conscious, I immediately joined the guys getting the gear out, hoping I could find a few dry sleeping bags. I'd completely forgotten about my shoulder until Levi caught me by the arm and a jolt of pain shot through it.

"Fuck, forgot all about that," I muttered as I looked to Levi.

"Figured you had," Levi replied. "Let me take a look."

I hesitated, thinking I didn't need to bother. Levi rolled his eyes. "Don't be stupid, man. It's cold and wet, and you need to get that bleeding stopped. It's not bad, but your shirt's wet. Under the best scenario, we've got a few hours."

I grumbled, but I wasn't stupid, so I consented to Levi peeling my shirt out of the way to clean and bandage the wound on my shoulder. It wasn't bad, but I could probably use a few stitches. For now, butterfly bandages held it together. Once we had Jesse and Fred squared away with some sleeping bags to keep them warm, we dug out some food while we waited.

It was hours later that the rain let up and we heard the distinct sound of a helicopter approaching. Levi and I set off flares in the misty light and waited as the helicopter settled to the ground beyond the edge of the trees. Amelia was about all I could think about once I knew everyone was okay.

Chapter Thirty-Three
AMELIA

I walked quietly from my cabin out into the adjacent field, tossing cracked corn along the way once I got past the driveway. A flock of sandhill cranes frequented the field every summer. Several pairs nested here as well. I loved that they came back year after year and sweetened it for them by scattering cracked corn every few days. I reached the edge of the small pond and tossed what was left in my small bucket along the edge of the water. A few cranes lingered a short distance away. It was late evening with the sun resting low on the horizon above the trees. The air was chilly with the rain just now letting up. I paused by the pond and took a steadying breath. The air felt washed clean by the rain. Fireweed was starting to bloom towards one side of the field. In another few weeks, every open space nearby would be awash in fuchsia with the wild weed flowering in abundance over most of southcentral Alaska.

The internal peace I'd worked so hard to cultivate after the turmoil when everything blew up before with Cade was difficult to find these days. I felt ridiculous at how easily Shannon had manipulated me again. All she'd done was imply it somehow meant something that she knew Cade was out of town. I didn't like seeing this side of myself again—the side that had driven me to bolt the doors around my heart and mind to anything that might brush against Cade. I didn't know how to balance loving him the way I did, being vulnerable, and also somehow retaining a sense of internal sanity.

It'll be better when he's home. It's just 'cause you're missing him like crazy. Yeah, but his job means he'll come and go a lot. You have to deal with that. You can't keep being this crazy about everything.

I sighed, my eyes drawn above to a pair of sandhill cranes flying down to land beside the others. If only humans could mate without so much fuss. Sandhill cranes mated for life, and as far as I could tell, they managed to do it without much drama. I laughed to myself, considering that I had no clue really. There could be tons of crane drama. Drama aside, they faithfully flew to the field every year and nested, taking good care of their baby chicks until it was time to fly south for the winter.

Meanwhile, I felt like an idiot because I couldn't keep my shit together. The bland, easy-going nature of my relationship with Earl might've made my heart ache for what I didn't have, but there was none of what I felt now. I'd tied myself in mental knots over Shannon's tiny hint, based on not much of anything. Then, when I'd managed to think straight again, all I did was miss Cade. I'd been working like a maniac since he'd been gone to keep myself from going batshit crazy inside. I'd worked so much, we'd gone from being behind schedule on the latest project to ahead of schedule.

I took a last look around the field and returned to the house. The cranes were pretty tolerant of me walking in and out of the field, but they stayed to the side when I did, so I liked to give them their space. Once I was inside, I kicked off my boots and started peeling off my clothes. Despite the rain, Lucy and I had worked through the day. As such, my jeans were damp, along with everything else. My skin was chilled and clammy. I tossed my clothes in the washer and hopped in the shower.

When I stepped out a few minutes later, finally warm all the way through after turning up the hot water so high it nearly scalded me, my phone was ringing. Not thinking much of it, I dried off and pulled on a pair of fleece pants and a sweatshirt. I needed warm and comfortable tonight. My phone started ringing again. I strode across the living room to snag it off the kitchen counter as I was running a brush through my damp hair. Glancing at the screen, I didn't recognize the number, so I didn't bother to answer.

The ringing stopped, only to start again. "What the hell?" I asked aloud, although no one was around to hear.

"Yes?" I asked sharply when I finally gave in and answered.

"Am I speaking with Amelia Haynes?" a man's voice asked.

"How about we start with who you are?" I countered, prickly and annoyed.

"This is dispatch at Fairbanks Fire & Rescue. We're calling about your fiancé."

I felt as if I was falling, my stomach hollow as if I'd dropped from a great height. My heart started pounding rapidly, and I felt sick. My knees gave way and I collapsed onto the back edge of the couch.

"Ms. Haynes? Are you still with me?" the man asked.

I swallowed and gave my head a little shake, trying to clear the buzzing sound in my brain. I felt lightheaded and strange, and I didn't even know what was going on. One thing I did know: someone calling from Fairbanks Fire & Rescue could only be connected to Cade, and it couldn't be good.

"Yes, I'm here. Just call me Amelia," I managed to reply.

"Oh good, thought I lost you there for a minute. I'm calling about your fiancée, Cade Masters. Let me start by letting you know he's okay. I can guess you might get concerned when I told you where I was calling from," the man said, his voice calm, clear and reassuring.

Hot tears pressed against the backs of my eyes, and my breath came out in a whoosh. I hadn't been able to form a thought about anything, but I'd been terrified something bad had happened, so knowing Cade was okay at least made it so I could breathe. "Okay, okay. Thank you for letting me know that," I said, my words coming out in a shaky rush.

"Of course. I'm Ed, by the way. Feel free to interrupt, okay?"

When he didn't continue, I realized he was waiting for me. "Okay."

"Mr. Masters and half of his crew were in a plane crash. Everyone survived, but right now they're waiting to be medevac'd out."

My stomach started churning like mad, while my heart kept up its banging rhythm. "How long do they have to wait? Is Cade hurt?"

I managed to hold myself to two questions out of the hundreds I had. It didn't escape my notice that Ed appeared to believe I was Cade's fiancée. That odd detail sent a curl of warmth around my heart. I didn't know who told him that, but I liked it.

"We've sent one helicopter out, but they can't bring the full group back due to weight and the space needed to stabilize two passengers who sustained more serious injuries. Mr. Masters is waiting with the rest of the crew until we can return again."

Relief washed through me. That meant Cade didn't have serious injuries. As soon as my mind absorbed that, I jumped ahead.

"How long will that be?"

I heard the panicky edge to my voice and didn't even care. It was approaching seven in the evening. If he wasn't flown out soon, I knew that meant he'd be spending the night out there. Rationally, I knew he slept in the wilderness all the time. If there were ever any group equipped to deal with crashing in a plane in the Alaskan wilderness and carrying on without missing a beat, it would be hotshot firefighters. Hell, they could just as easily hike back than wait for help to arrive assuming they were in good enough condition to hike. Those rational thoughts didn't dent the worry galloping through me.

"We're hoping tonight, but it may not be until tomorrow. With the fire, all of our medevac helicopters are tied up. There was another emergency out in the fire field as well. We're also dealing with significant visibility issues due to fog. The crew assured us they were equipped to make it through the night if needed. Mr. Masters passed along your name and insisted we call you since they're located outside of any cell reception."

I choked back my tears. It didn't matter what I told myself intellectually. I was scared to death knowing Cade was out in the middle of nowhere—literally—and might be spending the night in the wet cold.

"Is he injured?"

"As far as I understand, the crew members who remained behind sustained only minor injuries. Unfortunately, I don't know any more than that. I'll be calling Mr. Master's parents next. He asked we call you first and told us to tell you not to worry."

A sharp laugh escaped—a hurt, worried laugh that couldn't believe Cade would think I could manage not to worry.

"I'm sorry. I didn't mean..."

"It's okay, ma'am. Mr. Masters can tell you not to worry, but I make these calls like this often. I can imagine you'll be worried. Our rescue crew did check everyone over, so they considered him stable enough to stay put until they can return if that helps ease your mind at all."

I could hear the sound of ringing and beeps in the background of his call and realized he likely needed to move on.

"I'll do my best. I'm sure you need to go. Is there a number I can call for follow up if I need to?"

Ed quickly recited a number for me to call before ending the call. My arm dropped slowly. I stood where I was with my hips resting where I'd bumped into the back of the couch. My stomach was knotted with tension, and I felt buzzy and numb all over. All I could think about was Cade. I pictured him somewhere in the damp, cold wilderness. I knew he wasn't alone, but in my mind he was.

I didn't know how long I'd been standing there until my phone started ringing in my hand. Without thinking, I tapped the screen and answered.

"Amelia! It's Georgia. Honey, I've called your mother, and she's coming over to pick you up."

For a beat, I was confused, and then the gears in my brain started to move. Leave it to Cade's mother to swing into motion right away.

"Georgia, you didn't need to..."

Georgia cut right in. "Honey, you don't need to be sitting at home alone worrying about Cade. I'm worried too, but he'll be fine. Rex and I are here, and we figure you might as well come spend the night here. Rex already called into the dispatch up there. I can't even believe they didn't call us sooner, but Rex says they probably have no idea Cade's his son."

I managed a semi-polite answer and got off the phone right before my mother arrived. Under normal circumstances, I'd have shooed my mother away. I was too abuzz with concern to resist and next thing I knew, my mother had bundled me into the car and driven us over to Rex and Georgia's place.

I wasn't thinking about much of anything clearly, but the second I stepped into their kitchen, it hit me. I had somehow managed to avoid coming to this home for the entire seven years Cade and I had been apart. Under the circumstances, that was nothing short of a miracle. Georgia was one of my mother's best friends. She'd been pretty upset about our breakup, but she'd let me have my space. I hadn't consciously set out to never come to this home, but somehow I'd pulled it off.

Walking into the sprawling log home tucked into the trees sent a wave of nostalgia crashing over me. I'd spent many an afternoon here in the early days of dating Cade when we were home from college in the summer. It was hot and heavy whenever we weren't in Willow Brook, but when we were home in the summers, we practically camped out at his parents' home. It wasn't that we couldn't go to my mother's, but there was more privacy here. In those heady days, all we'd wanted was privacy.

With my heart knocking in my chest, I tried to slow my breathing, but it was an avalanche of memories. So many hours spent here with Cade. My eyes scanned the room. His parents' home was a modern single story log home. The kitchen and living room had beams crisscrossing the tall ceiling. Georgia loved her plants, as such they were scattered about the area. Windows looked out toward Denali in the distance, but the mountain was shrouded in the falling darkness and fog.

My breath hitched. On the heels of the wave of memories, another wave of emotion crashed behind it. Cade was out in that darkness and rainy fog. A full hour had passed since I'd spoken to Ed from dispatch in Fairbanks. That hour meant Cade and whoever else was left behind with him would be staying through the night.

Rex, Cade's father, must've noticed my expression because he slipped a chair behind me just when my knees buckled.

I glanced up into his face and managed a shaky smile. "Thanks. I, uh…"

Cade had his mother's green eyes, but everything else was his father through and through. Rex shared Cade's chiseled features and rumpled brown hair, albeit in a more weathered face and with streaks of gray. His brown eyes crinkled at the corners with his concerned smile. He squeezed my shoulder and sat down beside me at the kitchen table.

"You looked like you could use a chair," he said matter-of-factly. "Georgia, are you making coffee or tea?" he called over to Georgia who was already spinning around with two mugs of something in her hands.

My mother sat down beside me and rested her cane against the edge of the table. Georgia slid a mug in front of me, and I curled my hands around it. I'd been cold ever since I'd taken that call. Rex said something to my mother, which I didn't even hear. After a few minutes, Georgia was sitting across from me and reaching over to squeeze my hand.

"Hon, Cade is going to be just fine. Rex was able to talk to him through the radio earlier. I figured you'd be worried sick all by yourself, so why not come here, right?" Georgia asked, her warmth and concern so evident it was hard not to feel a little better.

"You talked to him?" I asked, my gaze swinging to Rex.

"Sure did. Just for a few. Maisie patched me in. Can't tie up the signal since it's the flight channel, but Cade said only two guys sustained serious injuries—the pilot and Jesse Franklin. The rest of 'em have some cuts and bruises, but they'll be fine. The fog up there's heavier than here. You sit tight, and we'll head up to Fairbanks tomorrow."

"We will?"

My mother laughed softly. "Hon, I mentioned that on the way over, but I think not much is sinking in."

I glanced to my mother to find her steady gaze on me. My mother was one of the strongest women I knew. I only wished I could be as strong as her. Physically speaking, I was, but my mother had an internal strength that had weathered her through my father leaving her with two young children at a time when she'd barely had two pennies to rub together. She'd not only pulled herself together, she'd given us an amazing childhood and paid for both of us to go to college. She'd taught me how to charge at life and grab it with both hands. What she hadn't taught me was how to love someone as hard as I loved Cade and stay sane.

The tension and worry balled up in my chest and stomach eased slightly. Rex wouldn't make light of it if there were something to worry about, that much I knew. As the chief of police for Willow Brook as long as I could recall, he was matter-of-fact and realistic no matter the circumstances. If he trusted Cade would be okay, then Cade would likely be okay.

"Figured we'd fly up tomorrow. We can fly from Anchorage to Fairbanks if there's room, or my buddy said he'd fly us up in his small plane if the weather's good. Way I figure it, Cade likely won't get home until day after tomorrow, so if you want to see him sooner, let's get up there," Rex said.

I nodded and took a swallow of whatever Georgia had handed me, just now noticing it was tea. Conversation carried on softly around me, and I gradually began to relax inside though my worry wouldn't stop until Cade was standing right in front of me, and I knew he was okay. Yet, it helped not being alone.

Georgia shooed me off to one of the guest bedrooms not much later with my mother promising to come by again in the morning with a change of clothes for me. Even though the tension coiled in every fiber had loosened slightly, I couldn't relax. Every thought looped back to Cade, and my heart ached with worry and missing him. Now he was somewhere in the dark wilderness—cold, wet and most definitely not with me.

Chapter Thirty-Four
CADE

I leaned my head against the seat with a sigh. I was fucking exhausted. Even under the best circumstances, camping through a night like last night would have sucked because it was cool and wet, and we certainly hadn't had the best circumstances. With the useless plane on the ground amongst broken trees, we'd set up camp nearby. Despite the fact it was raining, we'd opted against a campfire. The lingering threat from the massive fire only now contained was too fresh. We'd had a stroke of luck that the storage section of the plane had only minor dents and everything in it stayed dry.

Out of the six crewmembers who'd been on this second flight out from the fire, four of us remained behind for the night. The rescue helicopter could have held three total from the crew, but they needed space to keep Jesse on a stretcher. I'd spent the night rotating awake shifts with Levi, Thad and Jackson. Not that any of us slept much, but we needed to have someone up and moving in case any wildlife came by. We were in the thick of grizzly territory, which wasn't as risky as some might think, but we'd had enough to deal with already. A bear ransacking what little food we had would only make things worse.

I rolled my head to the side, catching Levi's eye. "How ya feelin'?"

Levi rolled his eyes. "Fuckin' tired. Can't wait for a shower and anything warm to eat."

I chuckled. "Damn straight." I tugged my phone out of my pocket and swore. At some point during the crash, my phone had gotten cracked and didn't work worth a damn other than to turn on. I hadn't even noticed at first because when I hadn't seen a cell signal, I figured it was because reception was so spotty out here. I'd later tried to check again to no avail and that was when I realized the phone would power on, but nothing else opened up. I hoped like hell dispatch had reached Amelia. My dad had assured me he'd let her know what was up as well, but it didn't change the fact I was concerned she'd be worried. I knew what worrying meant for her. She hated it, so she tended to get revved up inside. That never went well. I still hadn't gotten a blasted text to go through to her, so there was that to fester in my thoughts as well.

I watched the landscape underneath us with the steady thwack of the helicopter blades drowning out any other sound. The sky had cleared this morning, and a rescue helicopter came in to land not far into the morning. A crew from the National Transportation Safety Board was hot on their heels to do their thing—in short, a detailed investigation to report what we all already knew. The right plane wing collided with something in the fog and the plane crashed. The way the fog had cocooned us in the sky, visibility had been nil.

I'd been relieved to leave behind the investigators mulling about the area and was impatient to get to Fairbanks. I hated that meant yet another wait to be cleared to leave for Willow Brook. Since we'd been in a crash, I'd already received orders that we were to wait on site in Fairbanks to be interviewed for the NTSB investigation. All in all, more delay in getting to Amelia. It still wasn't sitting right with me that she'd gotten worried about Shannon's bullshit hints. Weary as I was, no matter the machinations of my mind, my eyes closed and I dozed off.

I woke with a start when the helicopter came down to land, setting down with a soft bounce. Within a few minutes, I was walking with the rest of the crew from the helipad into Fairbanks Fire & Rescue. All four of us were on a blind mission to the showers, and I could hardly be bothered to stop and chat with any of the local guys. Then, I heard Amelia call my name.

Disoriented, I spun around, quickly scanning the area. The waiting area here was busy with the station dealing with whatever usual issues at hand, along with juggling the presence of the NTSB investigators and a few extra hotshot crews passing through here to be sent out to the big fire. As such, there was a hum of voices and unfamiliar faces. I glanced around to find Amelia pushing her way through a few people toward the front doors. Her amber hair caught the sun glinting through the windows.

I forgot I was tired to my bones and cold all the way through. I dropped my bag to the floor where I was and strode to meet her. I didn't hear a word she said, although she was running on about something. I stepped to her, wrapped her in my arms and breathed her in. She shut up and buried her face in my neck. She smelled so good—like warm grass under the sun.

The sounds around us faded, and I simply held on. After a few minutes, someone tapped me on the shoulder. I lifted my head and glanced over to see my dad.

"Hey Dad. Didn't know you were coming up."

My dad flashed a grin. "Got the scoop you'd be tied up for a day or two and figured you might want to see your girl."

Amelia lifted her head, glancing between us and

throwing a wobbly smile in my dad's direction. "Thanks Rex."

My dad nodded, his eyes flicking to me. "You okay?" he asked, gesturing to my bloodied shoulder. The cotton had dried stiff, and the makeshift bandage Levi had put over the jagged tear was visible through the torn fabric.

Before I had a chance to speak, Amelia gasped and stepped back enough to check my shoulder.

I caught her hand in mine. "Hey, I'm fine."

Rex chuckled. "All I needed to know. I'll leave you two be. I'm checking in with an old buddy here at the station. Come find me when you're ready. I'm flying back tonight, but I booked a room for you two nearby."

I didn't even hear him walk away. I stared down into Amelia's amber eyes, trying to impart everything I felt in one look. "I missed you," I said, my voice rough with weariness and the depth of my feelings.

She caught her bottom lip in her teeth, letting it go with a sigh. Meanwhile, I knew I needed to be focused otherwise, but my body tightened and a jolt of need rolled through me. All because she bit her delectable lip.

"I missed you like crazy, but I can't think about it. Your shoulder's all bloody and we need to get it looked at."

She took another step back, reaching for my hand as if to drag me along behind her. Where I didn't know, but I knew Amelia would demand what she wanted. I curled my hand around hers and held firm.

"Wait," I said.

She turned back, and I reeled her in, pulling her flush against me. "Are you okay?" I asked gruffly, dipping my forehead to rest against hers.

"Am I okay?" she asked, her tone incredulous. "Of course, I'm okay! You're the one who was in a plane crash. You're walking around like nothing happened and..." Her breath hitched, her voice cracked, and she pressed her forehead into my chest, her breath coming in shudders.

"Hey, I'm okay. Really. I spend the night out in the middle of nowhere all the time. Usually with fire somewhere in the distance, so last night was no biggie," I said, sweeping my palm in passes along her spine.

"Yeah, but you've never been in a plane crash," she mumbled into my chest.

"Maybe so, but we're all okay."

"How come you're asking me if I'm okay?" she asked, still essentially talking to my chest.

Now might not be the best time to talk, what with people milling around us, phones ringing and zero privacy, but I wasn't walking anywhere without making sure we were on the level again.

"Because I got pretty stressed about you worrying about whatever bullshit Shannon said. I have no idea why she did what she did the first time, and why she would do anything now. You have to know that. I don't want you worrying about something so pointless," I said, my words coming out fiercer than I intended.

Amelia finally lifted her head, her eyes glistening. "I know it was bullshit. It's just you were gone and I missed you and I'm not used to us yet and everything feels big and intense so I freaked out."

Her words flew out in one long-running sentence. She paused and took a shuddering breath. "I'm sorry. You didn't need me getting all worked up like that when you were out there. I'll do better next time."

My heart squeezed in my chest, and I swallowed against the tightness in my throat. I lifted a hand and sifted it through her silky hair. After a beat, I managed to gather myself enough to talk. "You don't need to apologize. I just need to know we're good. I get it. Trust me, I get it. Seven years wasted all because of someone else's lies. I'm as susceptible as you. Hell, I hauled off and hit Earl. At the wrong time, if he said the wrong thing, well..." I paused and shrugged. "Don't be sorry. I just don't want you worrying about anything like that. I'm here and you are the *only* woman I think about. Hell, you're stuck with me, so you'd better say so if you don't want me."

Her eyes held mine, my heart thudding inside my chest hard and fast, before she closed the distance between our lips. In a flash, I forgot where we were and hauled her against me, sweeping my tongue inside her mouth. I forgot I was cold and so damn tired my legs were shaky. At the moment, the need bolting through me could've sent me on a marathon...as long as it involved Amelia bare ass naked tangled up beside me at the end.

"Get a room, would ya?"

Levi's voice broke through the fog in my mind, and I tore my mouth free from Amelia's. Her cheeks were flushed, and her eyes bright, and all I wanted was to be alone with her.

I glanced sideways to find Levi rolling his eyes. "Sorry to break up the fun, but we've got ten minutes in their locker room for showers. The medic is waiting to stitch you up too."

Amelia all but shoved me at Levi. "Go." She looked to Levi. "Make sure he sees the medic," she ordered.

Levi winked. "Of course. I'll bring him back all clean and stitched up."

I had to drag myself away when all I wanted was to stay right there with Amelia. If I hadn't known she'd boss me into the shower herself, I might've skipped out. As it was, I experienced a visceral ache stepping away from her.

Chapter Thirty-Five
AMELIA

I walked beside Cade down the hallway at the hotel. He'd been quiet since he'd returned from his shower to find me in the waiting area back at the station. His hair was still damp, and he had on clean clothes. Levi had hollered over to me that Cade was all stitched up, so we'd said our goodbyes to Rex and hopped in the rental car he'd arranged for us. I was relieved Cade was quiet because I was awash in nothing but emotion. My body was thrumming with need, and I could barely think past it.

I had the keycard in my hand, but had no recollection of our room number. I stopped in the hall. He glanced to his side, arching a brow. Sweet hell. With his damp brown curls, his green eyes and his body of nothing but muscle, I wanted to tackle him right here. My breath hitched and my pulse lunged.

"I don't know which room, do you?" I asked, my voice coming out raspy.

Cade's mouth curled at the corner as he shook his head. He reached for the key card and turned it over. It was blank.

Next, he tugged the receipt from the reception desk out of his pocket, scanning it quickly. "Room 34," he announced.

We stood beside room 30. In seconds, we were at the door to our room. Cade shouldered though, tossing his bag to the floor with a thump. The door barely closed behind me before he was on me, his mouth crashing to mine in a fierce kiss. Need spread through my veins like wildfire. I couldn't get close enough fast enough. He molded his body to mine, pressing me against the door, his hands roughly mapping over me as he yanked at my clothes. I was as rough and frantic as he was, tearing at his clothes. We stumbled away from the door, rolling against the wall in the short hallway as we left a tangled trail of clothing behind us.

The only pause came when Cade flinched, just barely, when I shoved his shirt off his shoulders. I tore my lips free. "Oh God! Are you...?"

"Fine," he bit out before his lips blazed a searing trail along my neck.

Goose bumps rose on my skin, chasing in the wake of his touch. I shoved his jeans down around his hips, biting back a groan at the feel of his cock as I curled my palm around it. His lips closed over a nipple, his teeth nipping just enough to send a bolt of need straight to my core.

My thighs were damp, my channel slick with need. He still had too many clothes on though, so I roughly pushed his jeans down. He palmed one breast in his hand and teased me, while his lips, teeth and tongue nearly drove me mad. He kicked his jeans free and spun around, lifting me high against him. I loved how strong he was, how it didn't matter that I wasn't exactly petite. He held me easily, injured shoulder and all. I'd completely forgotten about that with the feel of his cock against my folds. He took a step, bringing my back to the wall, and adjusted me in his arms.

With my legs curled around his hips, he paused, his dark green gaze locking with mine. My heart pounded wildly and my breath came in shallow gusts as I stared back at him, caught in the web of his gaze.

"Just so we're clear..." He arched his hips subtly into mine. Pleasure spiked through me, and I gasped. "It's you I want. Only you. Always you."

Despite being nearly lost in the thrum of desire and need, my heart felt so full I could burst. I couldn't do anything other than nod with my throat too tight for words. With his fierce gaze on me, he adjusted his angle and sank inside me in one swift surge. His forehead fell to mine on a ragged breath, and he held still for a beat. I could feel his heart pounding against my skin. After a moment, he began to move, slow, deep strokes into me. I was so wet, his motion was one endless slide and pull inside my channel. So close to release already, I tried to hold back. The pressure built and built, pleasure starting to ripple through me.

I curled my legs tightly around his hips and bit my lip.

"Don't," he murmured, his low voice a caress.

"Don't what?" I managed to gasp.

"Hold back."

With a subtle adjustment, he drew back and sank in to the hilt. I let go, my release uncoiling in a snap and hitting me so hard, I cried out sharply. He was right there with me on the next stroke. He went taut as a bow and let out a rough growl, his head falling into the curve of my neck as he shuddered and spent himself inside of me.

I thanked the stars I had a wall behind me and Cade holding me up because otherwise I'd have melted into a puddle. We remained like that for several long moments, our breath heaving. As my pulse slowed, I ran a hand through his damp, rumpled curls and traced along his neck to his shoulder, following the tidy square outline of the gauze over his stitches.

He lifted his head, catching my eyes. "You can only ask once an hour if I'm okay," he said, a sly grin curling the corner of his mouth.

I giggled. "I can manage that." I reached up to trace his brows, sobering as I looked at him. "I love you, and I went a little crazy missing you."

"Ditto." He paused, his throat working with a swallow and his gaze direct to my heart. "I know it's been a long time apart. Just focus on what matters—us. Don't let anything or anyone else tell you otherwise."

At that, he dipped his head and caught my lips in a quick, fierce kiss before tightening his grip on me and spinning away from the wall. "I think we need another shower."

Not much later, we were lounging on the bed with takeout pizza between us. I looked over at him propped on the pillows, his ridiculously muscled chest gleaming in the soft light, and thought maybe I could figure out how to love him as fiercely as I did and not lose my mind.

EPILOGUE
Amelia

I looked to the sky, dusky blue and dotted with clouds, and watched a helicopter descend to the helipad behind Willow Brook's Fire & Rescue station. The rotating wind created by its blades sent dust spinning in a circle across the open lot around the landing pad. The helicopter rocked on its landing, but settled quickly. It was a midsummer's late evening in Willow Brook. Cade had been gone a full two weeks up north at a wildfire. I was chomping to race across the lot to tackle him, but I knew I had to hang back until the pilot and the rest of the passengers disembarked.

A gust of wind blew my hair wild. I brushed it back to see Cade climbing off the helicopter. My heart started banging in my chest, and I forgot to hold back. Dashing across the lot, I collided with him just as he was turning and slinging his gear bag over his shoulder. Amidst six firefighters from his crew and the pilot, he stumbled when I flung my arms around him.

He caught me fast against him, his laugh muffled in my hair.

"Amelia, how many times do we need to remind you

you're not supposed to charge out here until it's clear?" the pilot asked.

I stepped back just enough to lift my head and looked over at Fred. Fred had been the pilot injured in the crash last year. He was still flying and had now added several routes for the Willow Brook hotshot crews to his rotation. He winked at me and then sobered. "Technically, I have to tell you that, so I'll just keep at it. Maybe someday you'll listen."

Cade's hand slipped down my back in a heated pass and gave my bottom a squeeze. "No she won't. She's more stubborn than me," he said with a chuckle.

I looked to Cade, colliding with his green gaze, and heat slid through my veins. Two weeks apart, and all I had to do was get near him and my body went wild. It was safe to say our chemistry wasn't wearing out yet. Fire season in Alaska, which stretched from spring to fall, meant he was gone every few weeks. The absences that had initially amped up my worry didn't anymore. They only made me a lust-addled wild woman when he returned.

My breath caught, and I almost forgot where we were. Until a balled up towel landed on Cade's head.

"What the hell?" he muttered as he yanked it off and glanced around.

Beck was approaching from the station and flashed a grin. "Just keeping the PDA to a minimum. How'd it go out there?" he asked, clapping Cade on the shoulder when he reached them and retrieved the towel he'd thrown at Cade.

Cade kept his arm tight around my waist as we walked into the station. I didn't pay a bit of attention to the conversation around us, while Cade updated Beck and the other guys. I soaked up the feel of his warmth and strength for a few minutes until I decided enough was enough.

"Okay, guys. Cade's done for now," I announced, curling my hand into his and tugging him away.

Beck arched a brow. "Sure you don't want him to shower first?"

I glanced over, scanning his chiseled features and rumpled brown curls. Truth be told, he was obviously in dire need of a shower. Dirt streaked his arms, soot streaked his face, and he'd likely slept in what he was wearing at the moment. Impatient though I was to have him all to myself, I reluctantly released his hand. "Fine. Maybe you'd like a shower first?" I asked, canting my eyes up to Cade.

He threw one of his devastating grins at me—my belly clenched and heat rolled through me—before nodding. "Might be nice. Give me five."

At that, he lifted my hand and dropped a kiss in the center of my palm before sauntering behind the rest of the crew into the back rooms at the station. I pushed through the door into the front and plunked down in a chair by Maisie's desk.

Maisie finished up a call and glanced my way. Her wide brown eyes were so similar to her grandmother's eyes I sometimes felt a pang from missing Carol's presence here.

"Waiting for Cade?" Maisie asked, managing sort of a smile.

"Yeah. Figured it was fair to let him shower first. It's not like he can't as soon as we get home, but it's been days, so..." I let my words trail off with a shrug.

What I was thinking wasn't polite to say in good company. Even with Lucy, I probably wouldn't say what I was thinking, which was I couldn't wait to get Cade naked and all to myself. I certainly didn't know Maisie the way I knew Lucy, so I wasn't about to say a thing.

Maisie's cheeks flushed slightly, and she nodded. "Yeah, they practically run to the locker room for showers when they get back. They didn't have a stopover in Fairbanks this time either, so..."

"They're filthy," I finished for her with a grin.

At that moment, the door from the back swung open and Beck strolled through. Beck managed the local crew for Willow Brook, which occasionally rotated out to the fires in need of hotshot teams, but they were back up rather than primary like Cade's team. Maisie's cheeks went from pink to cherry red, and she ducked her gaze down, suddenly busy typing something. I watched with interest.

Beck nodded in my direction and leaned his elbow on the counter. "You have a chance to submit those orders?" he asked Maisie.

Maisie's hair, pulled back in a slapdash ponytail with wild curls escaping willy-nilly, bounced when she nodded, but she didn't say a word, still typing away. Beck reached across the counter and snagged one of her curls, pulling it out and letting it bounce back.

By this point, I was fascinated. Beck took his duties as a ladies man seriously. He was ever cool and definitely didn't tease like this. He didn't need to, what with his black curls, flashing green eyes and body honed from steel. I might only get that crazy zing when Cade was around, but I wasn't blind.

Maisie whipped her head up just as Cade shouldered through the door. Whatever she meant to say, she bit her lip and stopped, her cheeks flaming and her eyes snapping at Beck. Cade barely glanced their way. "See you tomorrow, Maisie," he said.

At her nod, Beck spoke. "Meet us later at Wildlands?"

Cade glanced my way as I stood, sending my belly twirling with flutters, before looking back to Beck. "Nope. See you tomorrow," he replied with a wink as he strode to me, caught my hand in his and kept walking. Beck's laughter faded behind us as the door swung shut.

On the drive home with Cade's hand a hot brand resting on my thigh, I asked, "So what's with Beck teasing Maisie?"

"Ah. Saw that, did ya? Yeah, he's got a thing for her and doesn't even know it yet."

I whipped my eyes off the road to him. "Beck has a *thing* for Maisie?"

Cade chuckled. "Uh huh."

I forgot what I was going to say next when he slid his hand between my thighs. "Pull over," he said, his gravelly voice sending a hot shiver over my skin.

Fireweed blew in the breeze, an undulating wave of fuchsia flanking the highway. The sun was setting behind us, its light glinting in the rear view mirror amidst the streaks of red and gold flung across the sky. Denali stood in the distance, immense and regal. I knew precisely where he meant for me to pull over. A narrow dirt road just ahead that wove through the trees toward a lake hidden in the woods. This stretch of highway in Willow Brook was mostly empty of any homes with the tract of forest part of a dedicated land preservation area. We'd visited almost all of our old haunts in the year since we'd reconciled, yet we hadn't come down here. This used to be a place we made out, way back when we needed somewhere to go.

With heat sliding through my veins and all of my attention narrowed to Cade, I turned into the road, almost hidden amongst the tall grass and fireweed. Within seconds, we were hidden in the canopy of spruce boughs. I could barely think straight with him choosing now to tease me to madness by unbuttoning my jeans and sliding his hand inside. I managed to yank the car into a tiny parking area beside the lake and spun to kiss him.

In a tangle of limbs and kisses, we managed to get my jeans off and his shoved out of the way. Straddling him, I sank down, savoring the delicious stretch of his cock inside of me. I took him to the hilt and stilled when he said my name.

He trailed the backs of his fingers down my cheek. "I missed you," he said gruffly.

Emotion welled, and I had to catch my breath before I could speak. "Me too."

"I have an idea." His finger traced my lips, and I drew it in my mouth for a beat before he tugged it free, trailing a damp path down my neck and along my collarbone.

"What?" I choked out.

Because really, if I couldn't move soon, I might explode.

"Let's get married soon."

My heart flew skyward. "You mean it?"

"I don't know why we haven't yet. I was thinking about it while I was away. I figure if I miss you so damn much, I'd better make it official. I was kinda thinking there was no point in the whole wedding planning, but if you wanted..."

I held his face in my hands and peppered his cheeks and lips with kisses. "No wedding. It's not my thing. I hate planning and everything that goes with it—it's just silly. Let's just go to the courthouse and be done with it. We can have a big party after."

"Perfect," he murmured against my lips.

He leaned back for a beat, his eyes saying far more than words ever could. On the heels of a breath, he gripped my hips and lifted me, only to bring me sliding back down roughly.

Two weeks without him with my body at the very end of its restraint, my climax was upon me almost instantly. My head bumped the ceiling of the car. Held fast against him, I barely noticed.

CADE

I sat at the counter in the kitchen, staring out into the field outside. This land I'd once upon a time imagined would be mine with Amelia. That was another time, but the land was ours, the home was ours, she was mine, and I was hers. Her back was to me as she set the timer on the oven. After I couldn't wait to be inside of her and had to make do with a quickie on a back road, my eyes traveled over the flare of her hips and lush curve of her bottom. Her amber hair was damp from a shower, and her feet were bare. I was bone tired, but happy as hell.

The life of a hotshot firefighter wasn't glamorous. It was

damn hard work and dangerous to boot. I'd become accustomed to it long before I'd moved back to Willow Brook. I hadn't realized how fucking lonely I'd been in between stints out fighting fires. Coming home to Amelia felt so good and so right, thinking about life without her was bleak. That's what had gotten me thinking about marrying her finally. It wasn't that I'd doubted we'd be together, just that I hadn't thought much about making it official. The relief I'd felt when she didn't even hesitate was so profound, it reminded me how far we'd come in making our way back to each other.

I slid off the stool and circled the counter to wrap my arms around her. I felt her momentary jump, but she instantly relaxed against me and rested her head back on my shoulder, rolling to catch my eyes. "Yes?"

"Nothing. Just this." I dipped my head and caught her lips in a kiss.

***

Thank you for reading Burn For Me - I hope you loved Amelia & Cade's story!

For more smoking hot firefighter romance, Maisie & Beck's story is up next in Slow Burn. Beck is a flirt of the worst sort, and he drives Maisie absolutely crazy - in all the right ways. "A sensational, humorous, maddening, too hot to handle journey." Don't miss Beck's story!

Keep reading for a sneak peek!

Be sure to sign up for my newsletter for the latest news, teasers & more! Click here to sign up: http://jhcroixauthor.com/subscribe/

EXCERPT: SLOW BURN BY J.H. CROIX; ALL RIGHTS RESERVED

MAISIE

"Let me see if I understand you. Your cat got stuck in a tree, so you used your excavator to get him out?" I asked.

"Yes, that's what I said," Carrie Dodge explained, her tone exasperated.

I only knew Carrie's name because that was the second order of business whenever I answered a call at Willow Brook Fire & Rescue. Sadly, I still wasn't clear on what the nature of Carrie's emergency was.

"So, is your cat okay?"

Carrie's sigh came through the line. "Herman is fine. It's my excavator that's the problem."

When I answered a minute ago, Carrie had spoken so quickly, all I'd been able to piece together was something to do with a tree, a cat, and an excavator.

"Tell me what happened to your excavator."

I waited to hear the excavator had a name. Because this was Alaska and people named their tools and things like that here. I'd only lived here about two years, but I'd quickly come to learn some things were more important than others. Shiny cars—not so much. Excavators or fishing gear—worth their weight in gold.

"Oh, well, it was all fine at first. I got it right up by the tree, and Herman hopped in the bucket no problem. I lowered him to the ground and when I was turning it around, I forgot how close the ditch was and it fell in. I'm stuck inside," Carrie explained.

Rather calmly, I might add. This was the first mention a human was involved in this emergency beyond the role of an observer.

I tapped the alarm button on my desk. That would alert the crew on duty while I kept Carrie on the line until they arrived at her location. I'd already linked her GPS coordinates to our system. With rapid fire typing, I filled in a summary for the crew to see.

"Are you injured?" I asked Carrie, thinking to myself as long as she was okay, it was almost funny she'd neglected to mention her predicament this far into our call. I'd started out worried about the cat, then the excavator, when lo and behold, she was trapped in an excavator that had fallen in a ditch.

"I think so," Carrie said with a sigh. "Herman's looking at me through the window. My shoulder hurts a little."

"Do you mind if I get some basic info from you while the rescue crew's headed your way?"

"I suppose not," Carrie replied with another sigh.

I heard the garage doors opening on the back of Willow Brook's Fire & Rescue building and the sirens blare. Within seconds, an ambulance was racing past the front windows with a fire truck in its wake.

Carrie was remarkably calm and gave me her information with a few huffs here and there. I sensed she was more annoyed with her situation than with me.

I heard one of the crewmembers radioing to report they were within three minutes. I was the sole dispatcher for

Willow Brook Fire & Rescue. Though Willow Brook was a small town in Alaska, nestled in a valley in the foothills of the Alaska Range, its proximity to Anchorage and central location in the state had resulted in its Fire & Rescue crews being one of the hubs the state. Two interagency hotshot crews ran out of Willow Brook, along with a local crew. All three crews were fully trained for hotshot firefighting, which required intensive training and grueling work. Hotshot teams were sent to the most dangerous, remote fires in the country. Alaska's sprawling geography lent itself to plenty of fires. The Willow Brook teams mostly served Alaska, however they went wherever they were called. When they weren't deep in the wilderness fighting wildfires, they handled whatever came up here.

I chatted with Carrie until I heard the crew arrive. As soon as I ended my call with her, my other line beeped, indicating someone from the crew was calling in.

"Yes?"

"Hey Maze, what's the emergency? The cat or the excavator?" Beck Steel asked.

The moment he spoke, I got annoyed. Beck invariably annoyed me. I could practically see him grinning. I gritted my teeth and told myself I'd stay calm and professional.

"Neither. Carrie, the woman calling, is stuck in the excavator. Aren't you there?" I asked, proud of myself for keeping my voice perfectly level.

"Not yet. Crew says she's fine by the way. Mind telling me what this has to do with a cat?"

"Her cat was in a tree. She used the excavator bucket to get him out, and then the excavator tipped into a ditch," I explained.

"Of course. Because it makes perfect sense to use an excavator to get a cat out of a tree," he said with a low chuckle, his tone dry.

No matter what, Beck managed to get under my skin. Next thing I knew, I was arguing the point.

"It's not the worst idea. I mean, she got Herman out of the tree," I countered.

"Herman?"

"The cat. His name is Herman," I explained.

Another low chuckle from Beck sent my belly into a tailspin of flutters. I was hot and prickly all over and inanely arguing about the sensibility of using an excavator to get a cat out of a tree.

"Do you need anything else from me?" I snapped.

"Nah. Nice chatting, Maze," he replied.

The line went dead in my ear. I swore he called me like this just to piss me off. I shook my thoughts off of him, adjusted my headset and quickly entered everything from the call in our data system. I was unusually curious to see how Carrie was. Carrie's unflappable attitude got to me and made me want to know for certain she'd be okay.

I fielded a few more calls in the time the crew was out. They were still out when the top of the hour rolled around, and the call center in Anchorage took over duty for me to take a break. I still hadn't heard back from the crew and hoped Carrie was okay. I'd learned it wasn't the least bit helpful for crews to have me calling to check in, so I'd just have to wait. I powered down my computer and headed into the back area.

Two of our crews were out in the middle of freaking nowhere dealing with two different backcountry fires in Alaska. With the remaining crew out, the back of the station was deserted. I was feeling grubby after a morning changing the oil on the old truck Gram had left me. A side benefit to working at Fire & Rescue was access to the massive garage bays and tools galore. The crews handled all of their own maintenance. Amongst the three crews, there was a single female firefighter, Susannah Gilmore. She was also one of the few friends I had. Lately, she'd taught me how to change the oil in my truck, so I'd tried it this morning when no one was around. I kind of wished she wasn't out in the field because I didn't feel comfortable enough to ask any of the guys if I'd done it right.

Whether I'd changed the oil properly or not, I could use a shower. I'd been trying to figure out what to do about my broken hot water heater for over a week now. Cold showers sucked, so I'd been taking advantage of the showers here whenever I could. I preferred not to do so when anyone was around, so I planned to make it quick. The crew hadn't radioed they were on their way back yet, so I figured I had a little time.

Inside of a few minutes, I was savoring the steaming hot water pouring over me. The industrial hot water pressure here was phenomenal. I wondered if I could find a way to get this kind of pressure at Gram's house. My heart gave a little squeeze. It was technically my house because Gram had left it to me when she passed away, but I still couldn't seem to think of it as mine. It felt too much like her. I gave my head a shake and grabbed the soap, quickly soaping myself all over. I was rinsing the shampoo from my hair when I heard a voice.

"What the..."

I opened my eyes to see Beck standing in the entryway to the showers. I might've forgotten to mention Beck was the sexiest, most handsome man I'd ever known in person. There he stood in all of his glory. He still had his gear half on, but he'd taken his shirt off. His black curls were a wild mess, and he had dirt streaked on his cheeks and arms. His chest was a work of art—all glistening muscle, every inch of it practically carved from stone. His heavy-duty coveralls were hanging at his waist, tempting my eyes to look further down.

I was so stupidly staring at him, I momentarily forgot I was completely naked. Beck's eyes were wide, and his mouth hung open. He snapped it shut, and his eyes—those gorgeous, sinfully green eyes raked over me. If I didn't know better, I might've thought his gaze darkened with desire. But that was crazy, and I was naked.

BECK

Maisie Rogers stood in the showers—her delectable body bare for me to see. I couldn't have kept my eyes from taking a detour along every curve if I'd wanted to. Soap bubbles ran down her skin. I wanted to be those bubbles, caressing every inch of her skin.

Holy smokes. I was stuck right where I was. Her dark brown curls were wet and fell down around her shoulders, the water almost straightening them, but they were so wild, they couldn't be tamed. Her big brown eyes were like saucers. Oh, I'd have guessed Maisie had a body to die for, but she kept it hidden behind her t-shirts and jeans. Her breasts—oh my fucking God her breasts. They were round and bouncy with dusky pink nipples. I was perhaps ten feet away from her, so I couldn't be certain, but I was pretty sure her nipples got tight as I stood there and gaped at her.

Her waist curved in and then her hips flared out. My cock was hard inside of a second. I could instantly imagine gripping those hips, the soft flesh giving way, and sinking inside of her. Suddenly, she squeaked and spun around. If she thought that would help matters, nope. Her bottom was just as delectable as the rest of her. I'd never been one to love thin women. They were too, well, thin. I liked something to hold onto. Maisie had curves for days, plenty to hold onto.

"Do you mind?" she snapped, keeping her back to me.

Her voice was muffled by the water, but her snippy attitude came through loud and clear. Whenever she got like that with me, the urge to tease her was impossible to resist.

"I don't mind at all. Not one bit," I countered, letting me words drag out.

I was speaking the plain truth. I could stand there all day

and stare at her. If my cock had anything to say about it, I'd been doing a lot more than staring.

"Oh my God," she muttered. "Beck, please."

Just now, she didn't sound pissed. She sounded distressed, and it wasn't funny anymore. It suddenly occurred to me the rest of the crew would be in here any second. I didn't want anyone else to walk in on her like this. While I had always felt protective toward Maisie when she wasn't busy driving me nuts, now I felt territorial. I didn't want anyone else to see how fucking gorgeous she was.

"On my way out. I'll hold the crew at bay," I called as I forced my feet to move and walk out.

A while later, after I'd showered along with the rest of the crew, I made my way out front. I figured it would be best if Maisie and I went ahead and got the requisite awkward moment out of the way. I pushed through the swinging door out front to find her with her eyes studiously focused on her computer.

When she first started working here, she'd been pretty bitchy with the crews, but she was steady and professional on calls. So we kept her on, in part for that and in part out of loyalty to her grandmother. Carol Rogers had been our main admin person for decades. When she'd asked Sheriff Masters to hire Maisie, he'd immediately agreed. Maisie was an incredibly hard worker, and I respected her. I'd managed to keep the undercurrent of desire I felt for her at bay for a good two years now. Seeing her the way I just had wouldn't help matters.

I leaned my elbows on the counter surrounding her desk. "So Carrie Dodge is doing okay," I said, figuring if I started with something neutral and normal, perhaps it would just let us skip right past any awkwardness.

Maisie glanced up. "Oh good! You guys were there a while. What happened?"

I chuckled. "Most of the work was getting the excavator in a safe position so we could get Carrie out. She broke her collarbone and her elbow, so they transported her to the hospital. I'm still not sure how she pulled it off, but that damn excavator was on its side. If she hadn't been inside, it would've been no biggie, but she was pinned in the corner of the cab, so we had to be careful. Took some finagling."

Maisie grinned. "You shoulda heard her when she called. She didn't even mention she was in the excavator until a few minutes in."

"Doesn't surprise me a bit. Carrie's used to taking care of things herself. She was more pissed off she needed help than anything else."

"Well, I'm glad she's okay."

After that, Maisie looked back at her computer and fiddled with a bracelet on her wrist. Her teeth caught her bottom lip, worrying it. Oh fuck. My grand plan to breeze past this went up in smoke. Two years of trying to ignore my body's draw to Maisie and now I knew exactly how she looked—every glorious fucking inch of her.

"Didn't mean to surprise you back there. What the hell do you need to shower here for anyway?" There my mouth went, stumbling into the one topic I preferred to avoid.

Her cheeks got pink, and she kept her eyes trained on her computer screen. "My hot water heater broke," she mumbled.

Perfect. Something else to focus on other than Maisie naked and my hard cock.

"Well, why don't you get it fixed?" I asked the rather obvious question.

Her big brown eyes swung up to mine again. Damn. She was beautiful, and she appeared to have no idea. She had these wild brown curls she barely managed to keep tucked back in a ponytail paired with wide brown eyes and thick lashes that brushed against her cheeks. Her fair skin was scattered with freckles.

"I wasn't sure who to ask," she finally said.

"Come on, Maisie. Every one of us here would be glad to

help. How about I stop by tomorrow? I'll take a look and see if I can figure out what's wrong. If not, I'll help you install a new one."

She worried that bottom lip with her slightly crooked teeth, just crooked enough to make her smile downright endearing when she chose to let you see it.

"I'm worried it'll cost too much," she finally said.

Ah. I got it. Maisie was coasting by on what she earned, and I doubted she had any savings to speak of. Far as I knew, she was all alone since her gram passed away. My heart gave a funny thump. I ignored it.

"Let's start with seeing if I can fix it, okay?"

She met my eyes, her cheeks still pink, and finally nodded. "Okay."

I pushed off the counter and started to walk outside, her voice catching me right before I stepped through the door.

"Beck?"

I glanced back.

"Thank you," she said.

That's all she said, but she added a smile. It was all I could do not to turn around, walk straight to her and kiss her.

Available Now!

Slow Burn

Go here to sign up for information on new releases: http://jhcroixauthor.com/subscribe/

FIND MY BOOKS

Thank you for reading Burn For Me! I hope you enjoyed the story. If so, you can help other readers find my books in a variety of ways.

1) Write a review!
2) Sign up for my newsletter, so you can receive information about upcoming new releases & receive a FREE copy of one of my books: http://jhcroixauthor.com/subscribe/
3) Like and follow my Amazon Author page at https://amazon.com/author/jhcroix
4) Follow me on Bookbub at https://www.bookbub.com/authors/j-h-croix
5) Follow me on Twitter at https://twitter.com/JHCroix
6) Like my Facebook page at https://www.facebook.com/jhcroix

Into The Fire Series
Burn For Me
Slow Burn
Burn So Bad
Hot Mess
Burn So Good
Sweet Fire
Play With Fire
Melt With You
Brit Boys Sports Romance
The Play
Big Win
Out Of Bounds
Play Me
Naughty Wish
Diamond Creek Alaska Novels
When Love Comes
Follow Love
Love Unbroken
Love Untamed
Tumble Into Love
Christmas Nights
Last Frontier Lodge Novels
Take Me Home
Love at Last
Just This Once
Falling Fast
Stay With Me
When We Fall
Hold Me Close
Crazy For You
Catamount Lion Shifters
Protected Mate
Chosen Mate
Fated Mate

Destined Mate
A Catamount Christmas
Ghost Cat Shifters
The Lion Within
Lion Lost & Found

ACKNOWLEDGMENTS

I couldn't do any of this without the never-ending support of my husband. He even offers advice on cover models and titles with grace and humor! A bow of thanks to Yoly Cortez from Cormar Covers for her vision for this series. Amelia & Cade's story was a joy to write, yet nothing would end up the way it did without my editor. This book took some heavy lifting from my proofreader angels, all because I switched the point of view after I wrote the entire book. For catching those pesky details: many, many thanks to Beth P., Heather H., Janine, Terri E. and Terri D. - so gracious and patient, always making sure my books don't go out without their clothes on! My readers - you cheer me on, you send me funny emails, and you help me keep on writing. Thank you from the bottom of my heart.

xoxo

J.H. Croix

ABOUT THE AUTHOR

USA Today Bestselling Author J. H. Croix lives in a small town in the historical farmlands of Maine with her husband and two spoiled dogs. Croix writes steamy contemporary romance with sassy independent women and rugged alpha men who aren't afraid to show some emotion. Her love for quirky small-towns and the characters that inhabit them shines through in her writing. Take a walk on the wild side of romance with her bestselling novels!

Places you can find me:
jhcroixauthor.com
jhcroix@jhcroix.com

Printed in Great Britain
by Amazon